"Tell me, Jane. Does the fact that I kissed you bother you, or that we were interrupted by your colleague?"

"That kiss never should have happened," Jane said.

He gave her his most charming smile. "It should not have happened here, but it will happen again, Jane." He forced himself to drop his hand before he forgot his promise, slanted his mouth over hers and took what he wanted. "Only, next time it won't be at work. And it will be a proper kiss."

She gulped. "Proper?"

"Yes," he said with a wink. "A proper kiss from a prince." He lifted a strand of hair from her cheek. "And I promise it will be one you remember."

RITA HERRON

BRANDISHING A CROWN

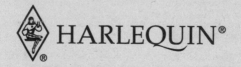

TORONTO • NEW YORK • LONDON
AMSTERDAM • PARIS • SYDNEY • HAMBURG
STOCKHOLM • ATHENS • TOKYO • MILAN • MADRID
PRAGUE • WARSAW • BUDAPEST • AUCKLAND

To my sister:
May she find her own prince one day...

Special thanks and acknowledgment to Rita Herron
for her contribution to the Cowboys Royale series.

ISBN-13: 978-0-373-74572-2

BRANDISHING A CROWN

Copyright © 2011 by Harlequin Books S.A.

Recycling programs
for this product may
not exist in your area.

This is a work of fiction. Names, characters, places and incidents are
either the product of the author's imagination or are used fictitiously,
and any resemblance to actual persons, living or dead, business
establishments, events or locales is entirely coincidental.

This edition published by arrangement with Harlequin Books S.A.

For questions and comments about the quality of this book please contact
us at Customer_eCare@Harlequin.ca.

www.eHarlequin.com

Printed in U.S.A.

ABOUT THE AUTHOR

Award-winning author Rita Herron wrote her first book when she was twelve, but didn't think real people grew up to be writers. Now she writes so she doesn't have to get a *real* job. A former kindergarten teacher and workshop leader, she traded her storytelling to kids for romance, and now she writes romantic comedies and romantic suspense. She lives in Georgia with her own romance hero and three kids. She loves to hear from readers, so please write her at P.O. Box 921225, Norcross, GA 30092-1225, or visit her website at www.ritaherron.com.

Books by Rita Herron

HARLEQUIN INTRIGUE

*Nighthawk Island
**Guardian Angel Investigations

CAST OF CHARACTERS

Prince Stefan Lutece—He has come to the U.S. to make trade agreements between his small island nation, Kyros, and America, but someone wants him dead. Who can he trust?

Jane Cameron—This sexy forensics specialist knows everything about processing crime scenes, but nothing about matters of the heart.

Lieutenant Ralph Osgood—Jane's superior and the head of her CSI unit believes Stefan and the COIN members are in the States on a fishing expedition to improve their military efforts and knowledge about bombs. How far will he go to prove he is right?

Prince Thaddeus Lutece—Stefan's brother wants his home, the island of Kyros, to remain a resort instead of a site for oil drilling, and he wants his brother to go through with the marriage his father has arranged to Princess Daria El-Shamy. Would he hurt his brother to stop the trade agreement from going through and to ensure Stefan agrees to the marriage?

Jihad Issam—The head of Kyros's tourist trade opposes oil drilling on the island, claiming it will ruin the country's idyllic setting and environment. Would he kill Stefan to keep his country from venturing into mining?

Prince Butrus El-Shamy—Princess Daria's brother is against the arranged marriage. But what are his reasons?

Hector Perro—Stefan's chief aide and loyal friend—or is he?

Edilio Misko—The head of Stefan's security team; can he be a mole?

Fahad Bahir—He's coordinating the security teams for all the royals.

Danny Harold—This news reporter seems to know more than he should; where is he getting his inside information?

Chapter One

"Stefan, if you would simply return to Kyros and marry Princess Daria, our problems would be solved. In exchange for the marriage, King Nazim El-Shamy has agreed to give our nation as much financial and military support as we need to fend off Saruk."

Prince Stefan Lutece sighed as his private jet began its final descent into the Wyoming airport. "Father, you know I have other plans for Kyros." And for himself.

And an arranged marriage was not on his agenda.

Saving Kyros from being swallowed by Saruk, the larger militant nation nearby, however, was.

But he didn't intend to succumb to his father's outdated means, or force his people to be swallowed into the folds of another nation. He wanted to utilize the oil on their land which could make them financially independent. That was the prime reason he'd joined COIN, the Coalition of Island Nations in the Mediterranean, and the purpose for his trip to America now.

And as far as marriage—if he ever indulged it would be with a woman who stirred his passions, not a woman like Daria who although physically beautiful, possessed a coldness in her eyes that chilled him to the bone.

"If this summit meeting goes as planned," Stefan continued, "and the coalition succeeds in making the trade agreements with the U.S., Kyros will prosper and gain independence without becoming indebted to King Nazim or Saruk."

The sound of the plane's landing gear rumbled, the plane tipped slightly, then righted, dropping altitude. Stefan glanced out the window at the rugged Wyoming land, the white-tipped mountains, the acres of untamed prairie land, and momentarily missed the lush tropical beauty of his own country.

Kyros, with its century-old ruins and stone temples, was rich in culture and history. With tourism as its main industry, the island was picturesque, boasting plush green foliage, colorful gardens, and inviting private resorts nestled along the Mediterranean coast.

But the island had been forced to become a

member of the EU, and with the euro so strong and with additional import costs, fewer and fewer people could afford the exorbitant costs of vacationing on the remote island.

He and his people had discovered several untapped areas prime with oil, though, that could turn around their economy.

"You know Thaddeus and I are both opposed to polluting our nation with mining," King Maximes growled.

"I do know that, Father. But as I've explained countless times, my team of experts has devised a way to minimize the waste and pollution to the environment." It was a major breakthrough, which he intended to use as a selling point to the summit.

"Do not sign anything until you discuss it with me and Thaddeus, Stefan." His father began to cough. "Remember I want what's best for our people."

"So do I, Father. And the COIN compact is what is best."

Stefan gritted his teeth as he ended the call. He felt his blood pressure rising. He and his father and brother would never agree on politics, but with his father's illness, an illness he was forced to keep secret to prevent Saruk from pouncing on them at a vulnerable moment, he was the new leader.

And he'd be damned if he'd allow Thaddeus to deter him. The spoiled brat did not want to make the tough choices but he wanted the glory—and their father's inheritance.

Suddenly streaks of yellow, orange, red and gold filled the distance, the brilliant sunset momentarily capturing his interest. Below him the desert with its spiny cactuses, sagebrush and tumbleweed reminded him of the ghost towns of the old West he'd seen in American motion pictures.

As the plane soared closer to its destination, mountain peaks jutted toward the sky and the desert gave way to hundreds of acres of ranchland, a winding river, and a valley filled with smaller ranches, wildlife, farmland, and green pastures where cattle and horses grazed.

Sheik Amir Khalid had chosen the meeting spot, claiming the Wind River Ranch and Resort was both sophisticated and full of grandeur, and if the sight below him was any indication, the description had not done the place justice.

Unfortunately he was not here for pleasure, but business.

He sipped the last of his scotch, then leaned back and watched the sunset fade as the plane touched down. Seconds later his cell phone beeped, indicating he had a text message.

Grimacing, he checked the text, half expecting it to be his father, yet hoping it was one of the leaders of the other COIN nations confirming their meeting place.

Instead a warning appeared on the screen, YOUR LIVES ARE IN DANGER. DON'T TRUST ANYONE.

His chest clenched with worry. He and the other royals were well aware that their arrival might cause trouble. Both anti-American sentiment and the fear of terrorists had been prevalent reactions when they had first announced the summit.

Who had sent this message? Was it a real threat?

The plane skidded to a stop, and a drop of perspiration slid down his temple.

It did not matter. He had to contact his security detail and the other COIN members and alert them that they might be in danger.

FORENSIC EXPERT Jane Cameron slumped onto the tattered sofa in the break room at the crime lab, sighing in disgust at the special news feed of the royals' arrival in Wyoming. Cameras panned the airport where the private jets for the dignitaries were landing. Security and police had roped off areas to fend off the nosy spectators, disgruntled citizens protesting the summit, and the swooning single women who wanted to sneak a peak at a real prince and sheik.

"Every girl's fairy tale—she'll grow up and marry a prince one day," Ralph Osgood, her boss at the crime lab, muttered sarcastically. "How about you, Jane? You got stars in your eyes?"

"Hardly," Jane said with a smirk. Fairy tales didn't come true.

She glanced at the newspaper photograph on the desk. Prince Stefan Lutece was clad in his prince's robe and crown, Sheik Khalid in his traditional robe…

Damn. Even if fairy tales did come true, a man like Prince Stefan wouldn't bother with a second look at a plain Jane like her.

Not that she was in the market anyway. She liked her life just fine. She had her job. Control of her own remote. The environmental issues she supported.

"Today marks a monumental day for Wyoming," Danny Harold, a cutthroat news reporter, stated interrupting her thoughts. "The Wind River Ranch and Resort will serve as host to a week of meetings that promise to help bring peace and economic security to the smaller nations of COIN as well as offering innovative and financially beneficial trade agreements to the U.S."

Jane poured herself a cup of coffee and stirred a massive amount of sweetener into the cup. Everybody in the world was in a tizzy over this damn summit meeting, raising the threat level for travelers and locals to a high. Hell, for the last week she'd worked around the clock checking out suspicious crime scenes that police suspected might be terrorist threats. Thankfully they had been bogus, but the possibility of problems was very real.

"Sheriff Jake Wolf, Wind River's local sheriff, is coordinating efforts between the various nations' security teams," Harold continued. "And now, here they come!"

Cameras focused one by one on the royals as they exited their private jets, each surrounded by a team of armed security agents in suits. In the background, protestors shouted derogatory remarks about terrorists, urging them to go home, while women and young girls shrieked at the sight of the princes and sheiks clad in regal attire.

"Sheik Efraim Aziz of Nudar," Harold announced, "...twin brothers Prince Sebastian

Cavanaugh and Prince Antoine Cavanaugh of Barajas… Sheik Amir Khalid of Jamala…and Prince Stefan Lutece representing Kyros."

While the crowd cheered and booed, and the security teams muscled through the throng escorting the royals to the scheduled press conference, Jane studied the individual men, silently admitting that they were all very striking.

Sheik Efraim Aziz, clad in a galabiyya and embroidered hat, had dark hair and eyes and looked to be in his late thirties. The twin princes of Barajas, Prince Sebastian and Prince Antoine, were over six feet with brown hair and wore trousers with shirt length robes. She'd heard that both had military training. Sheik Amir Khalid was slightly younger, in his early thirties with black hair. From what she'd heard, he had suggested Wyoming as the summit meeting destination because of an earlier visit. His hat was a kufi skullcap, his galabiya colorful.

Then her gaze fell on Prince Stefan, and for the first time in her life, her stomach fluttered. Not a girl to let a man turn her head, she was shocked at how her pulse jumped and her body tingled.

Prince Stefan had jet black hair that matched his impressive tailored black suit. His prominent cheekbones and patrician nose boasted of a Greek heritage and made him look regal as if he should be the poster boy for all royals worldwide.

Or as if he was a Greek god.

And when the camera focused on him, his piercing green eyes gleamed with an intensity, an air of authority and intelligence that made her want to climb inside his mind.

Yet those piercing eyes scanned the crowd with suspicion.

Suddenly he leaned over, spoke to the security agent beside him, and panic stretched across the guard's features. A second later, security agents surrounded the prince, then whisked him toward a limo while other security teams did the same with the remaining royals.

She tensed and tried to pan the crowd for suspicious characters. Something was wrong. Had the dignitaries been threatened?

STEFAN HATED to stir panic amongst the royals and forgo the initial press conference, but the moment he'd shared the text message, his chief of security Edilio Misko had contacted Fahad Bahir, Amir's personal chief of security agent and the head of security for the COIN compact. Fahad had canceled the press conference. Security had also insisted the men immediately be transported to the resort.

Stefan despised being forced to slink away like a coward when he was a military man at heart and could defend himself, but he had no weapon now, and he had to remember that he was representing his nation. This deal was far too important for him to dismiss even the smallest hint of trouble.

And worry that this threat would impact their meetings consumed him. Efraim was already on the verge of pulling out of the deal.

Surrounded by Edilio and five other security agents, Hector Perro, Stefan's chief aide, herded him toward the limo. Edilio pushed Stefan inside while shielding him with his own body. The security team surrounded the vehicle, each scanning the area for questionable characters.

Shouts from disappointed fans and protesters echoed from behind the gates as the limo driver drove toward the exit. Police had blocked off the parking lot as well as streets, and a pair of police cars led the entourage of limos as the collective group left the airport.

A mob of protesters lined the front gate, news station reporters and helicopters circled like vultures, and anti-Muslims waved American flags voicing their opinions.

Stefan frowned.

Even though he lived in the Mediterranean and Middle Eastern nations surrounded him, he failed to understand the hatred. He had valuable ideas which could benefit Kyros and the U.S., and he refused to allow either country to deter his mission of peace.

"I am sorry you did not get to hold the initial press conference," Hector said quietly. "I understand how important this trip is to you, Prince Stefan."

Stefan glanced out the window at the passing scenery. Night had descended, yet moonlight streaked the horizon, giving the rugged farm and ranchland an ethereal feel. Alpine meadows and Aspen forests filled his vision. Elk, deer, antelope, wild horses, cattle, mountain goats, and prairie animals roamed in their natural setting as if life had been turned back a century to a much simpler time.

A time before hatred and war and pollution.

"We must find out who sent this message," Stefan said quietly, "determine if it was in fact a threat, and if so, discern what the person who sent it might know."

"Yes, Prince Stefan," Hector said. "Edilio is trying to trace the origin of the message as we speak."

They passed an impressive sprawling ranch called the Seven M, then passed the Wind River reservation which jutted up to the resort property. Finally the driver veered down a side road and Stefan noted signs indicating the Wind River Ranch and Resort. The two-hundred acre secluded resort was situated on a working cattle ranch, a concept that intrigued him.

Yet this beautiful state was also troubled with pollution from their oil drilling. An area in which he possessed expertise and a problem he intended to rectify.

The main resort guest accommodations appeared as the driver wound up the drive. A sense of welcome engulfed him at the rustic charm, and the floor to ceiling windows and skylights with their majestic views of the mountains.

Minutes later, his security team ushered him through the enormous lobby, which boasted massive stone fireplaces and cozy seating nooks, to a large conference room where the other COIN members joined him.

"I'll see that your luggage is stowed and your suite properly prepared," Hector said, then excused himself.

Stefan nodded, then greeted each of the royals in turn while a staff waiter uncorked champagne and passed it amongst them.

"We have much business to attend to," Amir said. He gestured toward Stefan. "Stefan has alerted us that he received a warning not to trust anyone while here. We do not take this warning lightly. Yet we must forge ahead unscathed by the hostility of those who oppose us."

"Here, here," Sebastian said, then raised his champagne flute for a toast.

The men clinked glasses.

"The summit begins tomorrow, but tonight is for us to relax." A broad smile filled Amir's face. "I chose this resort for its privacy, beauty and charming hospitality. It would be shameful if we did not become acquainted with the area and partake of the amenities offered."

"I for one, am looking forward to those amenities," Stefan said with a devilish grin. "And something the locals call Shoshone lamb and navy beans."

The men laughed.

"I think a massage might be in order." Antoine rolled his shoulders. "The long travels seem to have created a kink in my neck."

More laughter followed as the men chatted about the possibility of attending an American rodeo, trout fishing, and hiking. A waiter appeared announcing dinner, and they were escorted into a private dining suite. Crystal chandeliers, a massive oak table, ornate molding and a picturesque view of the winding river added ambience to the artistically presented array of appetizers, meats, vegetables and desserts.

Stefan lacked a sweet tooth but tried each item displayed, his belly bulging from the fine cuisine. After dinner, drinks were served in a ballroom where they actually mingled with other guests. Stefan was surprised at the warm welcome, his earlier worries dissipating as the drinks and conversation flowed.

Efraim approached him, cognac in hand. "Amir has arranged a limo to drive us to the town of Dumont for some local flavor."

Stefan arched a brow. "Local flavor? That sounds interesting."

Efraim laughed. "Yes, no politics tonight. Our friend wants to play."

"Aren't you worried about the threat?" Antoine asked.

Amir shrugged. "If we let threats stop us, we would lock ourselves away for eternity and accomplish nothing."

Stefan nodded, although a frisson of alarm traveled up his spine.

Hector, always the fussy assistant, pulled Stefan aside. "Are you certain this is a good idea, sir? Perhaps you should remain here where it is secure."

"Amir is right. Do not worry so much, Hector," Stefan said. "This is my opportunity to see another part of this beautiful state and understand the people and their culture before visiting the oil drilling sites."

Hector's gray brows furrowed with concern, but Stefan dismissed him and hurried to join the others.

Dumont was located at the foot of the mountains and served as a point of departure for camping, fishing, hunting, mountaineering, and wilderness travel. They passed a national park as they drove into the town, then the city hall, a museum of Native American history, a casino, bed and breakfast, sporting goods shop, bike shop, Museum of the West, and various other businesses along the square.

"Dumont was named after a famous female expert gambler," Amir said as they climbed out at a rustic building where loud country music floated in the air. "Perhaps we should try a game of twenty-one?"

Sebastian and Antoine exchanged grins. "I intend to people watch," Sebastian said with a devious wink.

Stefan grinned. "You mean women watch?"

"Yes." Sebastian shrugged. "Purely research, mind you."

"Right, brother. We shall see what the west holds," Antoine said with a chuckle.

Stefan tensed as their security guards surrounded them. He would have preferred to visit the town uninhibited by the constant barrage of protectors yet knew it was futile to argue. Still, they made quite an entrance as the agents swept them in.

Locals stared and whispered, some snapping pictures with their mobile phones. A few women gawked and approached for autographs but the security agents warded them off.

Amir seemed preoccupied, as if he was searching the room for someone, and Stefan wondered if he had made friends on his previous visit to the town.

Country music blared, the locals participated in some strange dance called square dancing and clogging, but all the men were entertained.

By 2:00 a.m., jet lag and fatigue set in, and the men filed out, the late night patrons of the honky tonk having imbibed too much to gawk any longer. It appeared that alcohol softened the haze of animosity between the cultures. The fact that Stefan, Antoine and Sebastian had warmed to a few patrons and forced security to grant them some leeway hadn't hurt their cause, either. Efraim, on the other hand, continued to harbor anti-American sentiment.

Stefan yawned as the limo deposited them back at the resort. "Thank you, Amir, for showing us all a good night. If the remainder of the trip goes as smoothly, we will be leaving here with the COIN compact signed."

The other royals climbed out, each agreeing, but Amir remained by the side of the limo. "I have enjoyed it immensely, my friends. But I have an errand to do."

Stefan checked his watch. "At this hour?"

Antoine poked his twin brother. "You know our friend is a rebel, what the Americans call, a party animal."

Amir laughed. "You are right, I am not ready to end the party tonight. I will see you tomorrow at the summit."

Amir's security agent seemed irritated at Amir's decision, but allowed Amir to settle back in the car, then he joined him, and the limo disappeared again.

The security agents escorted Stefan and his friends to their private quarters, and Stefan dismissed Edilio so he could retire for the night.

Before going to bed, Stefan checked to make sure his notes for the next day's presentation were in order. His shirt was halfway unbuttoned when a pounding sounded at the door.

"Prince Stefan," Edilio shouted. "Sheik Aziz says it is urgent."

Stefan rushed to answer the door. Efraim bolted inside, his features contorted with worry. He grabbed the remote control and flipped on the television set.

"What is wrong, Efraim?" Stefan asked, his own heart suddenly pounding.

"A limo just exploded a few miles from here."

The special news broadcast burst onto the screen, cameras focusing on a burning vehicle. Smoke billowed toward the sky as rescue workers converged to douse the flames and save whoever might be inside.

"That limo," Efraim said in a choked whisper. "It looks exactly like the one that just dropped us off."

Stefan's blood ran cold.

The very limo Amir had left in only moments earlier.

Had Amir made it out alive?

Chapter Two

Jane's cell phone buzzed, jerking her from a restless sleep. She'd been dreaming about high school when she was a science geek and the popular kids had made fun of her.

They'd tied test tubes filled with condoms on her locker, then spray painted the words *virgin forever* on the front. The football team had thought it hysterical.

She had cried the rest of the afternoon.

The phone buzzed again, and she shoved the covers away from her face, cataloging the memory into forget mode as she reached for the phone. The ringtone signaled this call was work.

Not that she had many personal calls. That would require a personal life, and plain Jane Cameron didn't have one.

Her gaze landed on the clock as she answered the call. 2:50 a.m. What now? "Jane speaking."

"Jane, it's Ralph. Get your butt out to Snake Valley Road. We got us a crime scene."

"What happened?"

"Car bomb," Ralph said, his voice raspy as if he'd been running. Of course with his extra thirty pounds, he wasn't in the best of shape anyway.

"Injuries?"

"Yeah. One dead." Ralph wheezed a breath. "Don't know if there were other passengers, but them security dudes following them royals showed up. Makes you wonder…"

The hushed exit from the airport replayed in Jane's mind, and she instantly became alert. She could still see Prince Stefan's piercing green eyes searching the area as if he suspected trouble. Had he been inside the limo when it blew up?

She took a deep breath. "The royals were attacked?"

"Don't know for sure," Ralph said. "Sheriff Wolf's checking to see who was inside."

Stunned by how much it bothered her that the prince and his friends might have been murdered, Jane rubbed her hands over her eyes, then sighed.

She was not caught up in the grandeur of the royal blood like her own mother had been. For

God's sakes, Prince Lutece and his friends were just men. They put their pants on one leg at a time just like everyone else.

Except they wore robes of silk, had private valets to help them put their pants on, and held the future of entire nations in their hands.

But look where falling for a diplomat had landed her mother. Media attention and notoriety at first.

Then the man had cheated on her, made a fool out of her for all the world to see, and dumped her.

"Jane? If you're not up to this, I'll call someone else," Ralph said with his usual passive aggressive tone.

The hell he would. Ralph had been gunning to have her replaced ever since she'd been assigned to his team. He was major dark ages, thought women belonged in the kitchen waiting on their men hand and foot, and in the bedroom, catering to their every need, not in the lab or carrying a gun.

Not her style.

She could outshoot, outtalk and outsmart him, and she intended to prove that.

"Of course I'm up to it." Jane stood, shucking off her boxer pajama shorts and reaching for a pair of well-worn jeans among the pile of clothes on her floor. "I'll be right there."

Jane pulled on a T-shirt and boots, yanked her shoulder length hair into a ponytail, stuffed a baseball hat on her head, grabbed her weapon and rushed toward the door.

All week they'd been on standby in case there was a threat to the dignitaries, and now it looked as if their worst fears might have come true.

She jogged to her SUV, started the engine and peeled from the drive. The jeep bounced over the country road leading away from her cabin outside Dumont, slinging gravel as she sped down Snake Valley Road. The swirling blue lights of the sheriff's white Dodge SUV lit the sky as she approached the bomb site, the paramedics and fire engine adding to the chaos.

A news van—Danny Harold's station—sat parked next to the ambulance. As she climbed out, deputies were busy roping off the crime scene, and Sheriff Wolf ordered Harold behind the yellow tape.

Her gaze zeroed in on the charred body lying on the ground, and her throat closed. Was the dead man one of the royals, possibly Prince Stefan?

STEFAN AND EFRAIM rushed to the conference room to meet the other royals who had been quickly informed of the car bomb. "Was Amir inside the vehicle when it exploded?" Stefan asked.

Fahad Bahir entered, his face a mask of anger. "I believe so, but I've spoken with Sheriff Wolf and only one body was recovered. I'm on my way to the scene now to see if identification is possible."

"I will go with you," Stefan said. "I want to examine the bomb mechanism myself." Bombs were his expertise in the military. A bone of contention for some Americans, so he didn't exactly publicize the fact.

"The press, the police," Efraim said, wiping perspiration from his brow. "They will demand to know what happened. Where we were, if Amir was inside."

"And why he was traveling alone in the middle of the night," Sebastian added.

"Where *was* he going?" Antoine asked.

Tension stretched across the room as everyone traded questioning looks. Apparently their friend had not confided in any of them. "We must not alert the press or the summit members until we know if Amir survived," Fahad said.

"I agree," Stefan said. "It could create panic and interfere with the summit."

"We must also protect Amir's family," Efraim said. "There is no need to alarm them until we're certain what happened to Amir and if he is safe."

A chorus of nods solidified the agreement.

"That message I received seems even more suspicious now," Stefan commented.

Efraim shifted. "First, we have to determine if Amir was inside the limo at the time of the explosion. And we need a list of anyone who might specifically target Amir."

Fahad nodded. "I will work on that list and coordinate with all the security teams."

"Meanwhile we must devise a story to satisfy the media," Antoine suggested.

"We shall say Amir had private business to attend to," Fahad said. "That should mollify the local police until we discover what happened to Amir."

Stefan rushed toward the door, anxiety knotting his muscles. They'd come here on a peace mission, and if Amir had been killed, he'd find out who had set off that bomb and the reason.

"Stefan, keep us informed," Sebastian said.

Stefan nodded. "As soon as I know anything, I will call."

Fahad reached for his cell phone. "I'm going to alert security. Until further notice, each of you should remain in your quarters with your guards in place."

The men reluctantly agreed, and Stefan, Edilio and Fahad raced from the room. Minutes later, fear seized Stefan's chest as they parked at the crime scene, and he saw the remnants of the charred limousine and the dead man lying on the ground beside it.

Crime scene tape cordoned off the area. Thankfully, due to the late hour, there were no spectators hovering, only police officers and rescue workers. Although he immediately spotted the news van and broadcaster who had been at the airport earlier, and frowned.

How had this vulture found out about the attack so quickly?

A slender woman wearing a ball cap, jeans, and T-shirt that stretched across ample breasts caught his attention as she leaned over the charred body. Although not dressed in a police uniform, her demeanor, the way she stooped and meticulously examined the body, the subtle tilt to her chin as she surveyed the area, indicated she served in an official capacity.

America and their women, he thought with a mixture of awe and derision. One never knew where you might find one, how she would be dressed, and what man's job she might have acquired.

A tall, broad-shouldered man in a navy blue uniform shirt, jeans and sporting a wide pewter belt etched with a howling wolf design, strode toward them.

Stefan had been warned that the former sheriff of this county had been corrupt and rumors had spread to their security teams that other local law enforcement officers might be dirty as well.

What about this sheriff? Could he be trusted?

"Prince Stefan, I'm Sheriff Jake Wolf," the big man said with an accent that sounded lazy western, belying the tension lining his tanned face. "What are you doing here?"

Stefan shook his hand and introduced Fahad and Edilio. "We received word about the explosion. What have you found?"

Sheriff Wolf narrowed his eyes. "One body so far. We're searching the vehicle and victim for ID now."

"Was the victim in the driver's or passenger seat?" Fahad asked.

"Driver's seat." Sheriff Wolf indicated the surrounding land. "Got my guys searching to see if a passenger might have been thrown or crawled from the vehicle."

Stefan and Edilio exchanged a troubled look. Any life loss was tragic, but if the driver was dead and Amir's body wasn't inside the vehicle, he might have survived.

The woman hunched beside the victim pivoted to look up at him, and Stefan was suddenly struck by the startling shade of her eyes as she met his gaze. Not blue, not green exactly, but a mixture. Hazel, he thought as they flickered and changed in the moonlight.

Then his gaze slid down the ball cap to the dainty nose and full pink lips, and he swallowed hard. He'd expected a mannish woman below that cap, and granted this woman bore no makeup or feminine clothing, but his belly tensed with a sudden spark of attraction.

She might not be dressed for seduction, but a keen intelligence and innocence lay in her expression. And a sensuality that sent a sliver of desire straight through his groin.

"Prince Stefan?"

The soft timbre of her voice startled him even more. The gods, she had a bedroom voice. "You know who I am?" he finally asked.

A tiny smile curved her mouth, friendly at

first, then twisting with displeasure. "Of course. Doesn't all of America?"

He simply stared at her, speechless, and for the first time in his life, completely out of his element. He had bedded countless women in his years, yet this tomboyish female had his tongue tied in knots.

How could this be?

Fahad cleared his throat. "And you are, Miss?"

The woman rose, putting her almost a good half-foot below his six-two, her gloved hands by her sides. "Jane Cameron, forensics. I'm here with the crime lab to analyze and process the crime scene."

Fahad introduced himself and explained his presence. "And we are here to find out about this victim," Fahad said.

Fahad's words jerked Stefan back to the matter at hand, and he shifted his gaze to the dead man on the ground.

The last thing he needed was a feminine distraction. And the silky strands of hair peeking from the ball cap and spiraling around Jane Cameron's face and shoulders was definitely distracting.

"This man is not Sheik Aziz," Fahad said matter-of-factly. "He was the driver, Bahur Adler."

Jane Cameron planted her hands on her hips. Blast it. She also had curves.

"Forgive me, but under the circumstances, how can you tell?" Jane asked.

"The medallion around his neck, Bahur always wore it," Fahad said. "And he was missing the index finger on his right hand. He lost it in a childhood explosion in his country."

As if on cue, Stefan's gaze fell to the man's right hand. No index finger.

Stefan breathed a momentary sigh of relief that Amir might have survived. But if he wasn't here or in the limo, where was he?

JANE'S BREATH HITCHED as she stared at Prince Stefan. His green eyes hid a well of emotions, but she read fear, worry, caution and distrust.

Although for a second, those eyes had flickered with something else when she'd first looked up at him. He'd been surprised that she was a female. When his gaze had fallen on her mouth, she'd had to wet her lips with her tongue because they suddenly felt dry.

Then an odd look had crossed his stoic face. Not just surprise, but as if he might be pleased at what he saw. As if he found her attractive...

She swiped at a drop of perspiration beading on her upper lip.

Ridiculous. The heat and lack of sleep must be getting to her.

Not only would he laugh at the idea of her being attracted to him, but she didn't want any part of the limelight.

She'd had enough of that after her mother's death. Plain Jane in front of the camera, news reporters dogging her, strangers staring and prying, whispering and gossiping.

How could that odd little girl be the model-beautiful Genevieve Cameron's daughter?

"We'll transport this man's body to the morgue for an autopsy," Sheriff Wolf said, interrupting her trip down memory lane. "And we'll need contact information so we can request his medical records to verify his ID."

"Of course," Fahad said. "I will make the necessary calls immediately."

Jane noticed Ralph speak to the coroner as he arrived. Prince Stefan visually scanned the area where the vehicle had exploded. Remnants of metal, plastic and glass littered the asphalt, filling the air with the stench of smoke, charred metal and burned rubble.

"Did the driver suffer?" Prince Stefan asked quietly.

Jane studied the dead man's remains. "The

explosion probably killed him instantly, then the body burned post mortem."

The prince nodded. "Have you discovered evidence of another victim inside the vehicle?"

"Let me examine the limo and I'll let you know." She frowned. "Why the interest?"

Prince Stefan gave her a cautious look, then lowered his voice. "Our group used this limo earlier. It is important we know if this bomb was intended for us."

"You think you could have been the target?"

Prince Stefan shrugged. "One of our men took it after the rest of us retired. I need to know if he was inside." He touched her arm gently. "But we do not wish this news to be public. You understand, Miss Cameron? It could cause panic, and we do not know who we can trust."

His fingers sent a jolt of heat through her. A sexual kind of heat that she didn't want. Yet his words stirred caution. Had they received threats?

"Call me Jane," she said. "And don't worry, Prince. I dislike the media myself and will protect the investigation. They won't learn anything from me."

He studied her for a long moment as if debating whether or not to believe her, but finally gave a clipped nod.

More disturbed by his presence than she wanted to admit, Jane pulled away. "Now, I need to examine the vehicle. We might find clues as to the identity of the killer from the type of bomb and material used."

"And the detonation device," Prince Stefan said.

Jane raised a brow. "You know about detonation devices?"

A small smile lifted the corner of his mouth. "My military expertise was with explosives. But I'd rather you not make that public, either."

Jane bit back a sardonic smile. Dammit, he wasn't only sexy as hell, he was intelligent. She felt as if he'd lit some kind of fire in her belly. "I'm sure you wouldn't."

She spotted Ralph eyeing her and strode to the limo. Hopefully, she'd be able to assure the prince that this bomb had nothing to do with the royals, then he could leave, and she wouldn't have to deal with him again.

He was far too dangerous and tempting for a girl like her. Drooling over him would do nothing but lead to heartache, rejection, and put her in front of the media.

One place she never intended to be again.

STEFAN TENSED as Jane pulled away from him and rushed over to the limo to examine it.

Something had passed between them when he'd touched her. A charged heat that had surprised him.

One Jane obviously didn't feel. In fact, she seemed unfazed by him and unimpressed with his position.

He started toward the vehicle, but Sheriff Wolf stepped between him and Jane. "I'm sorry, Prince, but this is a crime scene. You'll have to stay back."

Edilio lifted a hand. "Sheriff, the prince is well educated in explosive devices. He can assist your people."

Sheriff Wolf scowled. "We can handle it on our own. Ms. Cameron is one of our best."

Jane pivoted from where she was examining the car, then crossed the distance to them. "The passenger seat in the front looks clean, but the backseat has blood on it.

Her expression turned grave. "I'm sorry, but it does appear that there was a second person in the car when it exploded."

Chapter Three

Stefan's chest constricted. Had Amir survived and escaped, or had he been blown to bits in the explosion?

Sheriff Wolf followed Jane back to the limo, and Stefan tailed him, hoping Jane was wrong. But Jane pointed to the seat and floor where she had sprayed Luminal, and Stefan saw the blood. Not just a few drops either. Enough to indicate someone could have been seriously hurt.

Sheriff Wolf spoke into his radio. "The blood suggests that a passenger was injured in the explosion. I want the search teams to cover a three-mile radius of the area."

Jane waited until he finished issuing his orders, then waved her lab assistant over. "Tomas, we need to find the blast point, then let's move out one foot at a time and collect everything we can find. Gum wrappers, pieces of metal, cigarette butts, glass—anything could have traces of the residue on it. Photograph and catalog it, then we'll take it to the lab for analysis."

The younger man nodded, hoisted his camera and went to work.

A balding man with a drooping left eye and a cheap suit approached Jane, then gestured toward Stefan. "What's he doing here?"

Stefan tensed at his surly tone, but Jane simply gave him a level look. "The dignitaries traveled in a similar limo earlier. Security team is just covering their bases."

Stefan hated compromising Jane by forcing her to lie, but security measures required it. He stepped forward and extended his hand. "Prince Stefan of Kyros. And you are, Sir?"

"Ralph Osgood, CSI and Jane's superior."

Stefan disliked the man immediately. Most likely he used his rank to bully Jane and anyone else around him.

Osgood stuck a toothpick in the side of his mouth and chewed on it. "Prince Lutece, you need to stay behind the crime scene tape. You could be compromising evidence."

Edilio stepped up to defend him, but Stefan shook his head, warning him to let him speak for himself. "As you suggest," Stefan said with more politeness than he felt.

Gritting his teeth, he stepped back behind the

crime scene tape. But what he really wanted was to examine the bomb himself.

He'd have to consult with Jane at the lab after she analyzed their findings.

Perhaps if he used his charm, she'd allow him to look at the evidence.

JANE FELT the tension radiating from the prince in his forced politeness to Ralph, but the smile he graced her with twinkled with an unspoken camaraderie as if he knew his good looks and smooth voice had won her over.

She had agreed not to share news with the press, but that was because she didn't trust the media not to mess up a good case.

Not because of the prince's mesmerizing green eyes.

Because she was a professional. And no one, not even the prince himself, would dissuade her from following protocol and doing her damnedest to solve this case.

Thankfully he moved behind the crime tape out of her direct vision, but she still felt his eyes watching her, studying her movements. Did he know something more about this bomb than he'd revealed?

If one of the royals had been inside when the

bomb ignited, why wouldn't he want them to alert the police?

Tomas was searching for forensics on the north side of the vehicle so she stooped to examine the underside of the car. The easiest bomb to make was one that involved gunpowder, a plastic bag and a wire. A blast-off mechanism was required, but the bomber could have used something as simple as a kid's rocket toy. He would have put it near the engine, then run wires from the ignition to the bag. When the car started, the electrical spark would ignite the gunpowder, which would have ignited the bomb.

Except the limo didn't explode when the engine started.

This bomb exploded mid-ride, meaning someone must have set a timer or been nearby watching to trigger the device.

She inspected the ignition, the engine and the gas tank and collected trace from all areas. The scent of burned metal and copper permeated the air along with the lingering odor of charred metal, burned rubber, blood and human skin.

Ralph was processing the car's interior, so she used her flashlight to scan the ground along the deserted road. A cigarette butt caught her eye, and she bagged it, then gathered several pieces of metal, wires and plastic that could have been part of the explosive.

When she glanced up, Prince Stefan was still trailing her with those intense eyes, and she had the uncanny feeling that he was holding something back.

A glint of metal suddenly flickered in the moonlight. She frowned, waved her flashlight across the sagebrush and prickly pears, and spotted something that looked like a cell phone in the midst of a patch of Indian paintbrush.

With her gloved hands, she knelt, pushed apart the scarlet leaves and foliage and retrieved the phone, then flipped it over. It could have belonged to the passenger from the limo. Maybe they'd lift some prints that would lead to the bomber.

Or at least the name of the passenger. Then they could look at motive.

Unless the driver had been the target.

They couldn't dismiss that possibility, although if this limo had transported the royals earlier, the more likely prospect was that the intended target had been all or one of the dignitaries.

She punched the connect button to make a call, but the battery on the cell phone was dead. The lab would have to do its magic, search for prints, the phone log history.

She bagged the phone and carried it to the evidence box. Prince Lutece's eyes flared with interest as their gazes connected, and he wove along the edge of the crime scene tape until he stood only inches from her.

"You found something?" he asked in a gruff voice.

She nodded. "A cell phone. Could be nothing, or it could have belonged to the missing passenger." She held up the bag and his jaw tightened.

"You recognize the phone?" she asked quietly.

A muscle worked in his throat. He was stalling. Debating whether to lie or how much to reveal.

Well, damn. Maybe the missing person was a friend of his. But she was not here to play games.

"Listen, Prince," she said, purposely inflecting sarcasm into the title. "I don't care what your position is. If you know the identity of the second person in the car, you need to speak up. Withholding information about a crime is a crime itself."

Anger sharpened his tone when he spoke. "I do not need a lecture on the laws of your country."

"And I don't need you breathing down my neck if you aren't going to cooperate. Do you know who this phone belongs to?"

He didn't speak for a moment. He simply breathed deeply, so deeply that the sound sent a tremor through her. He was afraid he *did* know.

And he also feared that he couldn't trust her.

The image of the panic on his face in the earlier news clip of his arrival rose in her mind in vivid clarity, sending a chill through her. He had received a threat. Maybe all of them had.

"I told you that I wouldn't reveal information to the press," she said in a low voice. "You have my word that I will be discreet."

"It is not just the media that concerns me," the prince said.

He didn't trust the police?

She didn't know how to assure him. Their last sheriff had been corrupt. Others had been rumored to be dirty, too, but she had no idea how deeply the corruption went or who might be involved.

And the prince's arrival, along with the other leaders of the Middle Eastern and Mediterranean nations, had stirred distrust and suspicion on numerous levels.

He stroked her arm, and her gaze fell to his hand. His fingers, his touch felt so gentle, yet his military background and leadership role indicated he possessed a steely strength and determination. That he would do whatever necessary to protect his people and his friends.

"We believe Sheik Amir may have been in the limousine," Stefan said in a tortured whisper. "But this news cannot be made public. And I do not want it shared with any of your law officials, even your boss."

Jane gave a clipped nod. She hated to lie to Osgood or other police, but she also understood the delicacy of this matter. Lives were at stake. "I just want to get to the truth," Jane said. "If your friend was involved, talking to me might help us find him."

"You will do your job," he finally said. "I just ask that you discuss any leads you find with me and get clearance with our security before you go public with information."

He sounded so sincere that against her better judgment, she agreed.

Suddenly the hairs on the nape of her neck stood on end, and her cop skills kicked in. Oftentimes criminals showed up at a crime scene and insinuated themselves into the investigation, so they could keep abreast of developments.

That and a morbid sense of watching the police scurry around searching for clues.

She turned and studied everyone at the scene and the surrounding area to see if anyone looked suspicious.

STEFAN GRITTED his teeth. He did recognize the cell phone. It was Amir's. Which meant the blood in the back of the limo most likely belonged to him, too.

Frustration knotted his insides. He did not like lying to Jane, but the earlier text made him extremely cautious.

Something about her tough-girl act impressed him. She wasn't trying to be coy or use him. She was simply doing her job.

A refreshing change from the manipulative, seductive women who had tried to lure him into bed—and into marriage—and earn a position by his side on the throne.

But he did not have time to analyze his odd attraction to her. Finding Amir was of utmost importance.

"Was gunpowder used as the explosive?" he asked.

Jane adjusted her cap. "I will release my results once I've analyzed the samples at the lab."

"But no signs of C-4 or another military explosive?"

Her eyes narrowed. "You do know explosives, don't you, Prince?"

He nodded. "Among other things."

Swinging the flashlight in a wide arc, Jane studied the angle of the limo, then shined the light on the edges of the asphalt next to the dirt.

Stefan followed the tracking light, and frowned as he noticed skid marks made by the limo. Then more tire tracks…

"There was another vehicle here," Jane said. "Either the bomber himself or a witness."

A witness would be invaluable. But if so, where was this person? "Perhaps someone found Amir and drove him for medical help." At least he prayed that was the scenario. Not that this person had kidnapped Amir.

"I'll have the sheriff check local hospitals." She traced a gloved hand over one of the tire tracks. "I'm going to take plaster casts of these."

"You can distinguish the make of the automobile by these impressions?" he asked.

Jane nodded. "If we look at the tread and wear, we can match them to a particular tire. There are databases that list which tires are installed from the factory on specific vehicles. And if there's a hole or cut in the tire, that makes it even more unique."

Stefan nodded, impressed.

"Let me get my supplies," she said.

He watched as she spoke with the sheriff, then rushed to the crime lab van. Seconds later, she returned with a camera and supplies. She took photographs of each tire track at a ninety-degree angle, then from various angles, then measured the width and the circumference of the wheels as well as the distance between the front of the tires and the rear tires.

She also knelt and collected samples of the rubber left on the asphalt and dirt and bagged it to transport to the lab.

Stefan noted the meticulous way she handled each piece of evidence, logging it into an evidence log to ensure proper treatment.

There were also shoe prints on the dirt by the second car. She measured and cast those as well.

Finally, she stood and returned to him, looking up at him beneath the brim of her hat. "We need to take a sample of your foot impressions."

He gaped at her, anger rising. "You cannot honestly believe that I had something to do with this bomb." It was a statement, not a question.

Jane gave him a sardonic smile. "You tell me. You were here within minutes of the crime. You refuse to be open with me. You've asked me to cover up anything I find from the press. I know that you recognize that cell phone." She sighed. "And you are a bomb expert. Do the math."

"There is no math to be done," he said, his voice hardening. "I am Prince of Kyros, here to make peace deals with your country and the limo my friends and I rode in earlier was blown up. I explained my reasons and you must accept them."

Jane planted her hands on her hips, her expression defiant. "I don't care who you are. I'm a crime scene investigator, and I'm going to find out what happened here. And whoever is involved is going to answer for this crime."

Stefan's cheeks burned. Edilio glanced up in concern from the car where he stood, and Jane's superior, Osgood, did the same. Furious, Stefan jammed his hands in his pockets to keep from shaking the insufferable woman and finding himself handcuffed by the local law like a common criminal.

Osgood strolled over, scratching at his arm where it appeared a rash lingered. "Something wrong?"

"I just explained that we'll need to take the

prince's foot impressions." Jane smiled tightly. "For elimination purposes, of course."

Stefan's gaze met hers. He saw the challenge. But heat rippled through the air, a charged tension that made his body burn with desire.

Edilio approached, his temper flaring in his eyes, and the reporter hovering on the scene started toward them.

Sheriff Wolf caught the reporter, though, before he could snap a photo.

"You insult the Prince, Miss," Edilio said in a harsh voice. "That is not acceptable. You must apologize."

Stefan raised a hand to warn Edilio to calm down. The last thing he wanted was to cause an incident with the local police. Or for this reporter to capture it. "No need for apologies, Edilio. Let Miss Cameron follow her protocol."

He gave Jane a seductive smile. "Take my prints, Jane. You will only prove that you are wrong about me. That even if you have a problem with me because I am a prince, that I am an honorable man, one you can trust."

THE SUBTLE INNUENDO in Stefan's voice sent a quiver up Jane's spine. She didn't really believe that the prince had anything to do with the bombing, and she had no idea why she'd baited him, but his presence totally unnerved her.

"I do not have a problem with you because you are a prince," Jane lied.

Rather because he was a man.

She didn't trust any man, especially a royal who could have any woman on any continent he desired. A man with wealth and power and people heeding his every beck and call.

She wanted him gone. Away from her so she could breathe normally again. So her fingers would stop sweating and her heart racing, and her mind would stop straying to dangerous avenues.

Like wondering what he thought about her. If he liked what he saw. If his hands were as sensual as they looked. And what it would feel like if he actually touched her with that sultry mouth.

Good grief. She was a moron to even think such nonsense.

"I'll need your shoes," Jane said.

"I will follow you to your lab and you may have them there," the prince said in a tone that brooked no argument.

"Fine." Jane grabbed the evidence box to transport to the lab, and strode toward her vehicle, but just as she crossed through the crime scene tape, the reporter shoved a microphone in her face.

"Can you tell us what you found? Who was in the car?"

Jane shook her head. "The department will issue a statement once the evidence has been processed and the victim identified. Now, please move, so I can do my job."

Stefan smiled as she elbowed her way past the leech. It had irritated him when she had used that tone on him, but amused him now.

"Prince Stefan," Edilio said. "Are you certain you want to cooperate with this woman?"

Stefan shrugged. "I think she will be useful in giving us information."

"Such a crass female," Edilio said. "I cannot fathom why some American women dress and talk like men."

Stefan's mouth quirked. *Crass* was not the word he would have chosen. Intriguing, sexy, smart. Not the type of woman he was accustomed to, but he would meet her challenge.

Still, responding to Edilio would only invite questions, so he refrained from comment.

Edilio drove and he tried to tame his libido as they followed Jane to the lab, parked and went inside. The crime lab was located in the brick courthouse in Dumont on the second floor and consisted of several offices and laboratories. Jane catalogued the evidence into their filing system, then settled at a workspace. With the late night hour, the lab was virtually empty, the halls reeking of pungent odors and chemicals.

"Find us some coffee," Prince Stefan said. "I will phone Efraim and update him."

Edilio nodded, then walked down the hall, and Stefan stepped into an empty corridor across from Jane's lab to phone his friends.

"The driver was killed," he told Efraim. "And there was blood in the backseat, but Amir was not inside."

"Then he could have crawled away after the explosion, and he still may be alive."

"It is possible," Stefan said. "But Amir's cell phone was discovered at the scene in the bushes. And there were tire tracks from a second car."

Efraim grunted. "There was a witness?"

"Either that or the second vehicle belonged to the bomber. If he saw that Amir was still alive, he could have kidnapped him."

Efraim cursed. "We must not let this information become known. Not until we discover the truth."

"I agree."

"I will handle making excuses to delay the summit," Efraim said.

"Thank you, Efraim. But do not give up on it. We will make this happen." Stefan's phone beeped that he had another call. "I am sorry, it is my brother. I should take this."

"Be careful, Stefan," Efraim warned.

"You do the same, my friend." Stefan connected his brother's call.

"Stefan," Thaddeus said. "We just received word that there was an attack on you and the COIN members. Are you all right?"

Stefan sighed. So much for staying out of the news. "I am fine." He contemplated sharing about Amir but decided to hold off. Sometimes his brother had a loose tongue. "And yes, there was a bombing but we were not inside the limousine at the time."

Thaddeus emitted a sound of relief. "Good. Now listen, Stefan. Father does not wish to frighten you but his condition is worse." Thaddeus's voice sounded anxious. "I think you should agree to the marriage with Daria and alleviate Father's worries about leaving our country in turmoil."

Stefan's fingers tightened around the handset. "I do not intend to debate this matter with you, Thaddeus. I have made my decision and it stands."

"But—"

Suddenly the lights flickered off, and Stefan tensed. A noise sounded. Footsteps. Something fell. Then a loud, shrill scream pierced the air, and Stefan's blood went cold.

Jane...

Chapter Four

Jane screamed. Someone was attacking her, had grabbed her by the neck…

She grappled for something to use to defend herself, but her fingernails barely scratched the surface of the metal table, and she stumbled. The lab was pitch dark.

Who the hell was on top of her?

She struggled, pivoting to try to see his face, but a hand closed around her throat, choking her. Frantic, she raised her knee and kicked backward, thrusting her foot into her attacker's shin.

He grunted and slammed his fist against the side of her head. Jane screamed again, flailing as she went down. Her head hit the corner of the table and pain ricocheted through her skull.

The darkness spun around her in a drunken rush, disorienting her. Then footsteps sounded. The back door to the lab swished open as if someone was leaving, but more footsteps pounded from the opposite direction.

Nausea clogged her throat as she pushed herself up to her knees and reached for the table edge to help her stand.

Suddenly a shadow crept into her vision, and she lurched into defense mode, threw her hands up and swung her fist toward her attacker.

The intruder caught her hands in his. "Jane, stop, it's me! Stefan."

Her breath rasped out as she fought the nausea again, but the voice registered.

The prince?

He took her by the arms and her knees buckled.

"Jane, are you all right?"

Jane sucked in a sharp breath. "Someone was here…attacked me."

The prince gently smoothed the hair back from her face. She could barely make out his face in the dark, but his eyes shone in the sunlight beginning to peek through the slats of the blinds.

He pulled his hand away, and gasped at the blood on his fingers. "The gods, Jane, you're bleeding."

"The lights…" she said. "See if you can flip

them back on. The evidence…I have to see if something is missing."

"Forget the evidence," he snarled. "You need medical treatment."

Edilio suddenly raced up. "Prince Stefan, are you all right? I heard a scream."

"I'm fine, but Jane was attacked. Search the building, and call an ambulance." Edilio nodded and hurried through the door.

Jane gripped Stefan's arm and tried to stand. "Find the lights. The breaker, in the hall. He must have tripped it."

"First, you need medical attention."

"No, I told you I'm fine," Jane screeched. "Now get the lights."

His long irritated sigh punctuated the tense silence. "Very well. But at least sit down."

The room swirled again, stars dancing behind her eyes, and she clutched him, hating to show weakness and determined not to pass out. She would not be some helpless female. She was a crime investigator for heaven's sake.

"You are bossy and insufferable," he growled. But his hands were gentle as he helped her make her way to one of the chairs in the corner of the lab. She collapsed against the vinyl seat and leaned forward with her head between her hands, gulping air.

"Jane." He brushed the back of her neck with his fingers. "Are you really all right?"

Gritting her teeth against the pain thrumming through her head, she reached up and squeezed his hand. "Yes. Now please, we're wasting time while he escapes."

He hesitated only another second before he raced from the lab. Jane blinked, intent on regaining her equilibrium, then ran her hand along the edge of the counter and found the phone. A second later she punched the number for security.

"Lock down the lab. We've been compromised. Suspect got away."

"Roger that." A brisk order to search the premises followed. "Do you need medical assistance?"

Jane hesitated. She hated to be babied, but she might need stitches. And documenting her attack was vital if they caught her assailant and went to trial. The prince's security called an ambulance. "Alert Sheriff Wolf. I had evidence from the explosion in the lab. It might have been compromised. I'm going to check now to see if anything is missing."

The lights suddenly flickered on, and she grimaced as she scanned the lab. Prince Lutece hurried in, his face a grim mask as he raked his gaze over her.

"You look like hell, Jane."

A sardonic chuckle escaped her. "I thought princes were supposed to be charming."

"Blood is not charming."

"You're right." She eyed the evidence bags she'd logged in and frowned. "Dammit. The cell phone. It's gone."

STEFAN GROWLED deep in his throat. The attacker stole Amir's phone.

Blast it. They might have lost a valuable piece of evidence that could lead them to the person behind the bomb attack.

And Jane—she looked so pale. Her eyes held hints of fear and pain, making his gut tighten with the need to soothe her.

Even worse, blood dotted her forehead, streaking her hair, reminding him that she'd been physically assaulted because of this case. Because of his friend.

A fact that infuriated him.

A fact that made him feel responsible.

He did not want to feel responsible for Jane Cameron, not a woman who seemed to snub her nose at his status.

Yet, he did want to alleviate her pain and fear.

His eyes fell on her hair, and his body hardened. During the attack she'd lost her ball cap, and her hair had come free of that ponytail. Her hair—it was golden brown and looked as silky as it had felt when he'd touched her earlier.

It also curled around her cheeks and made her look feminine and vulnerable.

Oblivious to his lustful thoughts, Jane pushed to her feet again but swayed, and he rushed to her. "Stay seated until the ambulance arrives."

She sighed. "I'm fine. I need to make sure nothing else is missing."

Stefan gritted his teeth.

He ached to pull her into his arms, hold her and comfort her. But the moment he stepped forward, she busied herself searching the evidence bags. "I hope security catches the bastard."

He bit the inside of his cheek at her colorful language. "Did you see the assailant?" Stefan asked.

"No, it was too dark." She angled her head toward him. "But I did manage to lift prints from the phone before the attack. I'll plug those in the database and see if I get a hit."

Footsteps sounded, and Stefan glanced through the glass partition and saw a man wearing a security uniform approaching along with

Edilio. Two paramedics entered behind him with Sheriff Wolf on their heels.

"Ms. Cameron," the guard said. "We searched the premises, but it appears your attacker escaped."

"Do you not have security cameras?" Stefan asked.

"I checked them but he must have tripped them when he flipped off the power," Edilio said.

A short, stout young man in a medic's uniform hurried toward Jane. "Miss, are you the one who was accosted?"

Jane nodded. "Yes, but I'm fine, really. Just a bump on the head."

"Let's take a look." He coaxed her to sit down, and Jane reluctantly allowed him to examine her head wound.

Sheriff Wolf moved inside, visually scanning the room. "What happened?"

"I catalogued the evidence into the system, then had started processing it when the lights suddenly flickered off." She winced as the medic cleaned the cut. "Then someone attacked me from behind."

The medic cleared his throat. "You might need a couple of stitches. We can transport you to the hospital—"

Jane shook her head. "Just fix me up with a butterfly bandage and I'll be right as rain."

"But you should go to the hospital and have a CAT scan," he argued.

A skinny female medic approached Jane. "If you don't stitch it up, you might have a scar."

"I don't care about a damn scar." Jane gestured toward the other medic. "I'm not going to the hospital. Now I have to get back to work so bandage me or I'll bleed all over the evidence."

The medic insisted she sign a medical release denying hospital treatment, then placed a bandage on her forehead.

Stefan wanted to throttle the stubborn woman, but realized arguing with her was futile.

"Can you identify your assailant?" the sheriff asked.

"No," Jane said. "It was too dark and he came at me from behind."

"Coward," Stefan muttered.

Jane swung her gaze toward him, and a small smile lifted the corner of her mouth.

"How do you know it was a male?" Sheriff Wolf asked. "Did he say anything?"

"His size, I guess. His hands were big." She twisted her mouth in thought. "And when I kicked him, he grunted, deep like a man."

Sheriff Wolf nodded. "Maybe he left his prints?"

Jane touched her throat absentmindedly, and Stefan's jaw tightened. The bloody animal had tried to strangle her.

"No use. He was wearing gloves," Jane said matter-of-factly.

"Did he take anything?" Sheriff Wolf asked.

Jane nodded. "The cell phone I collected at the crime scene." She examined the evidence box. "The samples from the road and car seem to be intact," she said. "And here are the blood samples from the car and the bomb particles. There were dozens of prints inside the limo, too."

"I'll file a report," Sheriff Wolf said. "Keep me updated on the evidence once you finish."

Jane agreed, then the sheriff and security guard left, and Edilio stepped into the hallway.

Stefan folded his arms. "My fingerprints will be among those in the limo," Stefan said. "And so will the other dignitaries traveling with me. As I said, we took that limo into Dumont earlier in the evening."

Jane's eyes flickered with sudden understanding. "I know you're concerned about the sheik. You think that you might all have been targets?"

Stefan could not deny the truth because Jane was too smart to already not have considered that theory.

"It is possible," he said.

"Then why do you want to keep it from the press and the sheriff?" Jane asked bluntly. "They might be able to help you."

There were not many people he trusted, and he did not offer that trust lightly. But this woman had nearly been killed because she was working this case, and perhaps because someone might have tried to murder Amir—and him and his friends.

He had to trust somebody.

"Because earlier I received a cryptic warning not to trust anyone."

Understanding dawned in her eyes. "That's the reason you all were whisked away at the airport."

He gave a clipped nod. "I will understand if you excuse yourself from this matter. I do not wish for you to jeopardize your life over a possible attack on my friends and associates."

Jane sighed deeply. "If you don't trust anyone, why did you just tell me about the threat?"

He lifted a hand to her temple and stroked

the bandage. "Because I think you are unusual. Dependable."

Jane made a sarcastic sound. "Careful, your charm is showing through again."

"I mean that as a compliment, Jane." His voice quivered as sexual tension thrummed between them. "I have never met a woman quite like you."

Jane's eyes darkened with sensuality, and Stefan's breath quickened.

He felt drawn to this sassy woman in a way he hadn't felt drawn to a woman in ages.

"I'm sure you're used to softer women," she said, her voice catching. "So you don't need to compliment me to persuade me to keep your confidence. I'm a professional."

Stefan's throat itched with laughter. He had never had a female speak to him so boldly—or insult him because of his mere position.

Did she really dislike him because he was a prince?

There was only one way to tell.

He trailed his thumb down her cheek, then lifted her chin, forcing her to look at him. "I do not offer you a compliment to earn your confidence, Jane." Needing to convince her that he found her spunk attractive, he angled his head and leaned closer to her. "And I do not give my trust lightly. But your honesty is appealing and refreshing, and…"

He was so close now he inhaled the scent of her body, the fragile earthy nuance of her skin. Hc felt her breath on his cheek, heard her breath hitch, then gently brushed his lips across hers.

"Well, well, Ms. Cameron," a loud male voice boomed.

Jane suddenly shoved his chest, and he jerked back, startled. He had been on the verge of kissing her thoroughly. And he did not welcome the interruption.

"I heard you lost evidence," the gruff voice said in disgust. A voice Stefan recognized as that insufferable boss of hers, Osgood.

Osgood sauntered toward them, arms folded. "And now, I understand the reason. You lied earlier. You obviously do have a thing for the prince."

Chapter Five

Jane's cheeks burned with humiliation yet her head was spinning from the wild unexpected feel of Prince Stefan's lips on hers.

Of all the damn times for Osgood to walk in.

"What were you doing? Making out with him while someone lifted evidence?" Osgood wagged a stubby finger at her. "Or did you lose it intentionally to cover for these royals?"

Jane sucked in a sharp breath at his accusation. Prince Stefan on the other hand hissed loudly, then strode toward her superior, a regal air of authority radiating from him.

"You are, what do you say in American—an imbecile and a baboon." The prince's nostrils flared. "Jane was physically assaulted while protecting the evidence she collected." He folded his arms haughtily. "Now I insist you apologize to her for your rudeness immediately."

Ralph's eyes widened with rage. "I do not take

orders from you, Prince Stefan." He straightened to his full height, but still the prince dwarfed him. "Miss Cameron is an employee of this lab, and you shouldn't be in here. Your mere presence could compromise any evidence collected."

Jane shifted restlessly. The situation was slipping out of control quickly. "Ralph, it's true that I was accosted. The prince was in the other room when he heard the attack, and came in to help so he hasn't compromised anything." Jane glared at him, irritated that he'd caught her behaving unprofessionally.

"Again I insist you apologize," Prince Stefan ordered stubbornly.

She clenched her hands by her sides. Didn't Stefan realize his reaction made her appear weaker in her boss's eyes? That it made her look guilty, as if something was going on between them when that idea was…ridiculous?

"Prince Stefan," she said between clenched teeth. "You do not need to speak for me."

"I beg to differ. A gentleman must defend a woman's honor," the prince said, his eyes teeming with anger.

"Perhaps the prince came to the lab as a diversion," Ralph muttered.

"That's ludicrous," Jane stammered. "He followed me from the crime scene."

Osgood's eyes glimmered with coldness. "Yes, it's odd that he was there, too."

She started to admit that the prince was worried about his friend, but caught Prince Stefan's warning look and snapped her mouth closed.

"You do not like the fact that my friends and I are in your country?" Prince Stefan asked.

Osgood heaved a breath. "I just don't trust your motives. Word is that you guys found uranium on your land and that your so-called business deals are a front. That you came to the U.S. to learn how to make nuclear bombs."

Jane swallowed hard as she studied the prince's reaction. She had heard rumors of those accusations, but had deemed the suspicions unfounded.

Osgood arched a brow. "Maybe this car bomb was just practice for a bigger agenda."

STEFAN HAD LEARNED the art of control while in the military, but this man taxed his restraint. Forcing himself to count to ten silently, he wrestled with anger. He wanted to smash the blasted imbecile's mouth with his fist.

But the reason for his visit to this country was too important to allow his personal emotions to cause him to act so rashly. He was here on a peace mission, and no one, especially this insufferable rude pig, was going to interfere with his purpose.

He glanced at Jane and hated the embarrassment in her eyes. He had caused her discomfort by kissing her at work. He also owed her an apology.

He would not compromise her again.

"Mr. Osgood," he said, utilizing the tone he reserved for politics "My friends and I are not in the U.S. to learn to make bombs. We are here, as we stated, to offer trade agreements and services that can benefit your people as well as ours."

"Actually it's Lieutenant Osgood, not Mister. And you have set up appointments to visit oil refineries in Wyoming," Osgood said in an accusatory tone.

"Yes, Lieutenant," Stefan replied. "But I have vital technology to offer your country, your state, technology that will allow your refineries to eliminate environmental hazards while processing the oil."

Osgood heaved another breath. "You and some of the others have military experience."

The statement implied ulterior motives, but Stefan could not deny information that was public knowledge. "Yes, in fact, my expertise is with explosives. So you see, I do not need your country to teach me to make bombs. I already possess that knowledge." He gave him a devious smile. "In fact, I could most likely offer you tips. Which, since I am here on a mission of peace and hold no animosity toward the U.S., I have no intention of doing, of course."

Osgood shifted onto the balls of his feet, his eyes darting around nervously. "If you think that's comforting to the Americans, you're wrong."

Jane cleared her throat. "Ralph, this is getting us nowhere. The prince has explained his reasons for visiting the U.S., and he saved me from the person who attacked me." Her voice was firm with conviction. "Now, I have evidence to process."

Ralph looked as if he was going to say more, but instead clenched his jaw. "I want to review each piece of evidence you find, Jane. If we discover the culprit behind the bombing, we have to make certain the arrest sticks."

Stefan frowned. He did not believe Osgood was worried about the investigation. He was a bully trying to throw his weight around.

But thankfully he left without saying another word, or Stefan would have told him so.

Jane crossed her arms, her expressive eyes brimming with emotions. "Prince Stefan—"

"Stefan," he said gruffly.

"Prince Stefan," she said, ignoring him. "You need to leave now so I can work."

"Jane." He lowered his voice to a sultry pitch. "I am sorry that I have caused you discomfort in your place of employment."

Jane's tumultuous expression softened. "I don't want to discuss it, Prince Stefan."

"Stefan," he said more firmly. Then because she was blushing again, and his pride insisted he know whether she had liked his kiss, he pressed on. "And what do you not wish to discuss, Jane?" He moved closer, lifted his thumb and brushed it across her mouth. Slowly, he angled his head, preparing for another taste. A real one this time.

Her lips parted into an O and a whisper of her breath rushed out. "Stefan…"

"Tell me, Jane? Does the fact that I kissed you bother you, or that we were interrupted by your pig of a colleague?"

"That kiss never should have happened," Jane said, pulling back.

He gave her his most charming smile. "It should not have happened here," he murmured. "But it will happen again, Jane." He forced himself to drop his hand before he forgot his promise, slanted his mouth over hers and took what he wanted. "Only next time it won't be at work. And it will be a proper kiss."

She gulped. "Proper?"

"Yes," he said with a wink. "A proper kiss from a prince." He lifted a strand of hair from her cheek. "And I promise it will be one you remember."

Her eyes sparkled with heat, and he smiled, satisfied to see that she felt the attraction humming between them just as he did.

Stepping back from her took grave effort. "Now, I will leave you to do your job and find this bomber. But I implore you to call me with your findings."

Jane nodded. "It would help if I had a sample of your friend's blood and fingerprints to compare with what I collected."

Stefan's stomach churned. "Very well. I will have the sheik's personal assistant send them to you. But please, Jane, I would prefer you not allow your superior to view the results."

"Stefan—"

"I know it is asking much and you could be risking your employment," he said thickly. "But this is important, Jane. Even if you believe you can trust this imbecile Osgood, he might share that information with someone disguising themselves as trustworthy."

She touched the bandage at her temple as if weighing his words, then finally conceded with a nod. "I'll do everything I can to find out who did this, Stefan."

His heart jumped at the sound of his first name on her tongue. The gods help him. This Jane Cameron was proving to be quite interesting.

But he had to return to his friends and see if they had news of Amir. Maybe Amir had somehow escaped the bomb and had found a way to contact one of them.

JANE'S BELLY FLUTTERED as Stefan strode from the lab. Dammit, the man had caught her off guard.

Why had he kissed her? Was he trying to prove a point? Trying to buy her confidence?

She had already given him her word that she wouldn't speak to the press.

So why had he promised he would kiss her again? His words echoed in her head, taunting her. *A proper kiss from a prince...*

What did he mean *proper?*

She shifted restlessly, disturbed by the heat flaring inside her belly. She didn't want proper. She craved something much more improper, something untamed and wild. Something she'd never had.

And she had tasted hints of it in that simple brush of his mouth across hers.

How far would he have taken it if they hadn't been interrupted?

She groaned and dropped her head into her hands. What was wrong with her? She knew better than to let a handsome, sexy man turn her head. Especially a charmer like Stefan.

No, she would stop this foolish thinking now. Falling for Prince Stefan would be as dangerous as throwing herself in front of a train.

She would solve this case, then he and his friends could finish their business and return to their countries where they belonged.

Her resolve intact, she focused on processing the evidence. First, she plugged the fingerprints she'd lifted earlier from the phone into the database, then ran them through AFIS, but as she expected didn't find a match.

The royals' prints would not be in AFIS. She'd have to wait for the security agent to send over the sheik's prints.

Next she analyzed the small metal and glass fragments she'd collected from the crime scene along with the samples of residue. An hour later, she had determined that gunpowder was used to ignite the mechanism, and that one of the pieces of wire she'd found had been attached to the engine. But another small fragment indicated the trigger, which she suspected had been set by someone nearby, and could have come from another car following the limo.

Had the bomber known that the other COIN members had already exited the vehicle before he triggered the explosion?

Debating that question, she analyzed the tire prints and plugged the samples into the system. The lab wasn't state of the art, but she had fairly decent equipment and the necessary program was available so she ran the tire tracks through the database.

The first set belonged to the limo. The next set were distinctly different, both in tread and width, and the right front tire had an imperfection that would make it distinct and easy to match if they found the make and model and located a specific car to compare it to.

She watched the program work as it analyzed her findings and smiled as the information spilled onto the screen. Technology was a miracle worker.

The second vehicle at the scene had been an SUV. An older model Chevy Suburban.

Now the more important question—had the car belonged to a witness or the bomber?

STEFAN PHONED Efraim and asked him to gather the COIN members for a meeting while Edilio drove him back to the resort. Early morning sunlight streaked the horizon, painting the ranchland they passed in shades of gold and orange, highlighting the rugged wilderness and beauty. Cattle grazed and horses galloped across the terrain, the earthiness of the setting reminding Stefan of the environmental issues he could bring to the table at the summit.

If they continued.

This attack would definitely hinder their business, but he refused to give up on the COIN compact. Doing so was tantamount to negotiating with terrorists, and he staunchly opposed allowing them that kind of power. He would make his mission a success.

He had to for his country and his people.

And he would do so without succumbing to a loveless marriage to Daria as his father desired.

Edilio parked and escorted him inside the facility, checking over his shoulder and constantly scanning their surroundings for security purposes.

Stefan rolled his shoulders as he entered

the conference room and headed straight for the coffee pot. Hector hurried toward him, his craggy face riddled with worry.

"Prince Stefan, you need sleep now. You have been up all night."

Stefan sipped the coffee, grateful for the caffeine. He had been in the military, had been trained to survive without sleep. "I am fine, Hector. I must speak with the COIN committee before I consider rest."

Even at his age, Hector's eyes sharpened. "What did you learn? Was Sheik Khalid hurt in the explosion?"

Stefan held up his hand as the others filed into the room. "Stay and I will explain."

Hector stepped to the side as the others entered, yet his presence comforted Stefan. Hector had been nothing but loyal to him. He'd assumed care of his father and him since Stefan was just a boy.

Efraim approached, followed by Antoine and Sebastian, their faces strained with anxiety.

"What did you learn?" Efraim asked. "Any news about Amir?"

"No," Stefan said with a sigh. He gestured for the men to sit, and Hector brought a tray of coffee for them. "The driver was definitely killed, but the police did not locate a second body at the scene."

Antoine pulled a hand down his chin. "They searched the surrounding area?"

"Yes," Stefan said. "The explosion occurred on a deserted street, and they searched a wide perimeter. Jane found a phone—"

"Who is Jane?" Sebastian asked.

"Jane Cameron," Stefan said, realizing he'd used her first name. "She is a forensics expert who was investigating the crime scene. She processed the limo and searched for trace evidence in and around the explosion."

Antoine accepted a mug of coffee. "The phone belonged to Amir?"

"It appears to be his," Stefan said. "Ms. Cameron needs a copy of Amir's prints and blood work for comparison. I will have Fahad handle the matter."

"She found blood?" Efraim asked.

"Yes." Stefan nodded. "Even if Amir survived, he was injured. And judging from the amount of blood, I would say seriously."

Worried murmurs rumbled through the room.

Stefan placed his coffee on the conference table. "There was also a second set of tire tracks at the scene."

Sebastian grunted. "What does this mean?"

"That there might have been a witness," Stefan said. "Someone who could have helped Amir."

"Or that car could have belonged to the bomber and he could have kidnapped Amir," Efraim pointed out.

Stefan cleared his throat but nodded. "There has not been a ransom call?"

"No," Efraim said. Sebastian and Antoine both shook their heads.

"How do we proceed?" Antoine asked. "Do we alert the police?"

"No," Stefan said. "I do not trust the local law enforcement officers. I followed Jane to the crime lab, but she was assaulted there, and Amir's phone was stolen."

Efraim muttered an unpleasant phrase. "I must point out that I anticipated problems here in America. Maybe we should cancel the summit altogether."

"No," Stefan said firmly. "We will find Amir and finish our business. But we must be careful. The police were the only ones who knew about the evidence Jane collected." He frowned. "Also, that reporter Danny Harold was at the scene."

"The American media are vultures," Efraim said darkly.

Antoine and Sebastian agreed.

"We need to identify where that bomb came from and who was behind the attack," Stefan said. "That explosion may have been intended for Amir, or it could have been meant for all of us."

"I will talk with Fahad, have him compile a list of Amir's enemies," Efraim offered.

Stefan's stomach knotted. "We should each make a list of our own. This attack could have been orchestrated by Americans or our own people, ones who oppose the COIN compact."

"Or it could have been personal," Sebastian said.

Stefan nodded gravely. "I have many enemies myself."

Antoine drummed his fingers on the chair arm. "Between the five of us, the list could be endless."

Stefan's cell phone buzzed, and he checked the number. Jane.

He snapped the connect button. "Jane?"

"Yes. I just talked to the sheriff. It's not good news, Stefan."

A muscle tightened in Stefan's jaw. "Tell me."

"Sheriff Wolf checked the local hospital, emergency rooms and morgue," Jane said. "No one matching your friend's description has been admitted."

Stefan's pulse pounded. Then where was Amir now?

Chapter Six

As soon as Stefan ended the call with Jane, his cell phone buzzed again. This time it was Prince Darek Ramat, a longtime friend to each of the men in the summit.

If he had heard of the bombing, perhaps he had information that would help.

He punched the connect button. "Stefan speaking."

"Darek. I heard of the attack, but the news is not clear here." Darek's shaky breath rasped out. "What is going on? Are you and the others all right? Was anyone injured in this car bomb?"

"Amir was the only one in the limo at the time," Stefan explained. "The driver was killed, but Amir's body was not found. We have not heard from him, so at this point, we are unclear whether or not he is alive."

Darek muttered a rare expletive, a sign of his distress. "If Amir was inside the limo when it exploded, how could he have survived?"

"I do not have answers yet," Stefan said. "The local police are investigating."

"Didn't they search the area?" Darek asked.

"Yes, of course." Stefan sighed. "They found Amir's cell phone. However, there were tire marks indicating another vehicle had stopped at the scene. It is possible there was a witness or that the driver helped Amir escape."

"Then he could be in a hospital somewhere close by?" Darek asked.

Stefan swallowed hard. "Police have checked hospitals and emergency rooms, but there has been no sign of him. And thank God he hasn't turned up at the morgue. But there is another possibility."

"He was kidnapped," Darek said matter-of-factly.

"Yes," Stefan said, the very idea grating on his nerves. "Although there has been no ransom call."

Darek released another expletive. "I cannot believe this is happening. I warned Amir that traveling to the States was dangerous."

"Yes, but we all thought it worth the risk."

He only hoped they did not regret it in the end.

JANE WAS SHOCKED at how quickly Stefan managed to have his friend's fingerprints and blood work sent to her. Fahad Bahir, Amir's head of security and the agent coordinating the individual security teams, personally transported the file and insisted on watching as she processed the information.

His intimidating manner and perusal made her feel jittery, a feeling Jane didn't like. This lab was her home, dammit, and she hated the way he filled the space. Tall with broad shoulders, and the body and harsh eyes of a bouncer, he looked threatening. Even more disturbing, she sensed he enjoyed intimidating her.

She lifted her gaze from the computer, and he was there, inches from her, his breath rushing down her neck, chilling her.

"What do you see?" he asked.

"The blood is a match to the blood on the seat," Jane said, lifting her chin and forcing herself to face him. Nobody made her back down. Certainly not this bully. "The prints on the phone matched Sheik Khalid's as well."

Fahad arched a thick brow. "And the tire tracks that belonged to the second vehicle?"

"An older model Chevy Suburban."

"What else can you tell me about it?"

Jane shrugged. She didn't understand why, but she'd rather discuss the results with Stefan instead of this brute. Still, he represented the royals, so if Stefan was in danger, she had to do whatever she could to protect the dignitaries. "Not much. Our lab is not high tech here, but the sheriff might be able to run it through the system and determine how many people own that type of SUV in and around the area." She paused. "Of course, SUVs are popular in this state. And if this vehicle belonged to the bomber, it's most likely a rental."

"But it is possible to trace its whereabouts?" Fahad asked in a thick accent.

Jane nodded. "Might take some time, but it's possible."

He glanced at the test tubes and slides she'd studied earlier and frowned. "What else have you learned?"

Jane leaned against the counter, debating how much to share. There was something about one of the particles she'd found from the bomb site that disturbed her. Something she didn't recognize.

Something that made her think military.

She had to talk to Stefan in private.

"I've told you all I know," Jane said. "If we had the sheik's phone, I could have checked his call log, determined if anyone had called prior to the bombing, if he received a warning or threat of some kind, but without it…"

Fahad's dark eyes roved over her. Suspicious.

Then he gripped her by the arms with such force that she winced.

"You do not speak to anyone about this matter, do you understand? Our security depends on it."

Jane glared at him, teeth gritted. "I understand. Now take your damn hands off of me."

His gaze locked with hers, and for a brief moment, she thought an apology might come. But he released her abruptly and strode toward the door. Then he paused with one beefy hand around the doorknob. "Beware, Ms. Cameron. My job is to protect the royals and I intend to do just that."

Jane gave a clipped nod, but held her breath until he exited. She watched through the glass window as he strode down the hall and stepped onto the elevator.

Then she grabbed the lab report and her purse and hurried toward the door. She had to talk to Stefan and see if he recognized this bomb material. She would not deal with that Fahad character again.

If this had been more than an attack on the sheik, if terrorists were involved, the danger might not be over.

STEFAN CONTEMPLATED his numerous enemies carefully before he listed them for fear of retribution and worsening relationships that were already on shaky ground once the prospects realized they were under scrutiny.

Yet Amir had been attacked and that attack might have been intended for the COIN members, so they could not discount anyone who opposed the U.S. meetings or had issues with one of the COIN members.

He jotted down the first name he thought of. Jarryd Isam, the head of the tourist trade for Kyros. Jarryd opposed the idea of oil mining on the island. Like Stefan's brother Thaddeus, Jarryd feared mining would ruin the tranquility of the resort areas and pollute the air. He refused to believe that Stefan's research team had discovered procedures to minimize the negative environmental effects.

Stefan had tried to convince him that the economic value would far exceed any negative effects, but to no avail. Jarryd hated the U.S. and opposed trade agreements with them.

Next on his list, Butrus El-Shamy, Daria's brother and the next in line for leadership of their country when Daria's father, King Nazim died. Prince Butrus was opposed to the arranged marriage his father wanted, and had other plans for their country's resources, none of which included saving Kyros or dealing with the U.S.

Stefan believed that Butrus had secret intentions of supporting Saruk if Saruk overtook the smaller nations of COIN. But now Darek had assumed leadership of Saruk from his father Kalil, Stefan felt less of a threat. Darek had been friends with him, Antoine, Sebastian, Efraim and Amir for years. Together, they would find a way to make peace and work things out.

There were others from each nation who opposed the summit, his own brother included, but no one stood out. At least no one he considered a physical threat. Thaddeus was more of a wordsmith than a violent man, and if he was following his usual pattern, was most likely sipping scotch while his harem of women doted on him. Money and name bought material things as well as personal and sexual favors, and Thaddeus preferred the pampered life.

Antoine, Sebastian and Efraim each handed him a list at least as long as his.

"I'll have Hector search through my correspondence and email for additional suspects," Stefan said. "I suggest you all do the same."

"Yes, right away," Efraim said. "Then we can assign our teams to investigate each name."

The men agreed, and Fahad gathered the

lists to make copies and pass amongst the individual security team leaders. Hector coughed,
and Stefan frowned. Hector was aging, and he'd
sensed the man's health might be starting to
fail.

"Are you all right, Hector?"

Hector's face blanched, and Stefan wished
he'd refrained. His loyal servant had always
hated having attention drawn to himself.

"Yes, Prince Stefan. Just a dry throat. Must
be the climate here."

Stefan nodded. Kyros did have the cleanest air
he'd ever breathed, the climate here drier. But
Wyoming breathed of wildlife and raw animal
energy that made him itch to ride across the
terrain undeterred by his country's problems.

An image of Jane Cameron's beautiful face
flashed into his mind, and he imagined her hair
blowing in the wind as she straddled a thorough-
bred and galloped across the land.

His body hardened at the image, and he
shifted, determined the men in the room not witness his reaction. Without seeing Jane and touch-
ing her, they could not understand the sexual
pull that gripped him each time he thought of
her.

Outside, Stefan heard the sound of a helicopter roaring above and glanced out the window. A

media chopper was circling the grounds. Blast. Was it that Danny Harold again?

Edilio had left to make a phone call but strode into the room. "Gentlemen, there is a protest march rallying outside the resort. It appears to be growing volatile. I suggest each of you retire to your quarters and remain there until the situation is under control."

Stefan clenched his fists. He strongly opposed retreating like a coward.

His friends grumbled similar complaints, but filed out, and Edilio approached him. "Prince Stefan, Ms. Cameron phoned that she is on her way. She claims she has evidence she needs you to examine."

Stefan's heart began to pound. What if Jane was outside in that mob?

JANE'S PULSE RACED as she spotted the mob of protestors, a mixture of antiterrorists, antiAmericans, Middle Eastern supporters, environmentalists and gawkers who simply wanted a peek at the princes and sheiks staying at the Wind River Resort. Shouts, curses of anger, vows of support, welcoming words, and hate words jumbled together, barely discernible with the roar of the helicopter above.

Sucking in a sharp breath, she parked, showed

her ID to security, then elbowed her way through the outskirts of the crowd, determined to talk to Stefan. In all her years and even with the notoriety her own mother had attained through her connections, she had never seen such a controversial group of people. Cameras flashed, the crowd pulsing with anger, resentment, violent undertones and…awe.

The sun beat down on her as she muscled her way past the mob. She had just reached the front glass doors when a security guard stepped in front of her.

"No one gets in now, miss," he said.

She flashed her badge. "I'm here to see Prince Stefan. It's important. He should be expecting me."

"Let me check." He punched a button on his radio, and static sounded.

"Who are you, lady? You here to protect the terrorists?" an angry man shouted.

Jane touched her badge. "Settle down, sir. These dignitaries are not terrorists."

"The hell they ain't," another man bellowed.

A big burly man in faded jeans with tobacco-stained teeth rubbed up against her. "Damn them foreigners."

"We don't want them here," a man who reeked of beer yelled. "They're trouble."

"Stand back," the guard shouted.

Unrest rippled amongst the group, the mob mentality escalating. Someone pushed another person, creating a domino effect. Jane felt the momentum as a stream of people lunged forward, smashing against the glass. The security guard reached for her arm to help her through, but another angry protestor shoved him, and he grabbed his baton and swung it up, then spoke into his mic.

"Everyone stand down or you're all under arrest."

The burly man who'd started the upheaval closed his hand around Jane's wrist in a steely grip. She struggled against him, but he jerked her so hard, her body slammed into his, then he tried to drag her through the mob. Suddenly the glass door slipped open, another strong hand yanked her by the arm, and she stumbled.

"Let her go," Stefan commanded.

"It's the Prince!" someone screamed.

The mob pushed harder, and Stefan twisted the man's arm, forcing him to release her. Jane flailed to keep her balance, furious and embarrassed, but Stefan dragged her inside and two security agents rushed to close the door and keep the mob at bay.

"Blast it, Jane!" Stefan barked. "You are going to get yourself killed."

Even though she was breathing hard, anger surged through her at his tone. She tried to swing around to confront him, but he coaxed her away from the door.

"Are you crazy?" she shouted. "I'm supposed to protect you, yet you come to the door when there's an angry crowd outside. You could have been attacked!"

Sweat beaded on his skin, and his eyes darkened with fury. "I was trying to protect you, Jane."

She glared at him, but her heart was pounding from the ordeal, and when he hauled her into his arms, she collapsed against him for a moment. Her shaky breath rasped out, and she clutched his chest to keep from falling apart.

Outside, the shouting intensified, people pounded on the glass doors, stamping wildly. Police raced around in an effort to corral the unruly group and prevent more violence.

Stefan closed his arms around her, stroking her back, and despite her best efforts, her bravado slipped, and she clung to him.

"Shh," he whispered against her hair. "I do not wish to see you harmed, Jane."

Jane sighed against him. Defeated. Tired. A little frightened.

He was a prince, after all. Maybe the most admirable man she'd ever met. Certainly the most noble and chivalrous.

And how long had it been since she'd been treated like a woman?

Heaven help her. She gave in to the temptation, and allowed him to comfort her. She would only do it for a moment, she promised herself.

Just a moment.

Then she would pull herself together and focus on the case before she made a complete fool out of herself and fell for Prince Stefan.

STEFAN'S HEART was beating so fast he thought it might explode. When he'd seen that baboon's hands on Jane, he had nearly come out of his skin with fury. He had never been able to tolerate anyone manhandling a female, and he certainly would not stand by and watch some slob maul Jane.

The stubborn woman.

He stroked her back, savoring the feel of her sweet curves against his. Her hair smelled like some exotic flower that grew on Kyros, invading his nostrils and sending a flare of raw longing through him.

But a loud noise startled him into looking up, and footsteps pounded. He spotted Edilio racing toward him, then coaxed Jane around the corner, out of the view of onlookers plastered to the glass doors.

Jane pulled herself together. "Stefan, I wanted you to look at this lab report and see if you can identify this particle from its composition."

Stefan narrowed his eyes as he studied the report. "I can't be sure, but it seems familiar. I could tell more if you allow me to look at it in the lab."

Jane nodded. "We can go back now."

Stefan took her arm, then turned to Edilio. "I am accompanying Ms. Cameron."

"You must have security escort you," Edilio said.

"I will be fine with Jane," Stefan insisted. "She will protect me with her weapon, will you not, Jane?" He gave her a teasing look.

Jane's lip curled upward into a wry look. "Of course."

Edilio stepped in front of him. "No, Prince Stefan. You will not leave without a security detail."

Stefan sighed, weary and hating to have anyone watch him with Jane lest they see his ridiculous attraction to her. But he would be a fool not to accept security—simply being with him might endanger Jane. And he could not live with himself if she were hurt because of him.

"Very well. Call Benito. I need you to start investigating that list of enemies."

Edilio nodded, and radioed for his second in command. Benito appeared a moment later.

"You cannot go out the front, Prince," Benito said.

Edilio frowned. "Take them through the back exit, Benito. I'll create a distraction."

Edilio headed toward the front.

Stefan held Jane's arm, and they followed Benito down a hallway, along another corridor, then through a gigantic kitchen and out the back door where two limousines stayed parked for use by the royals. He and Jane slid into one, and Benito took the driver's seat and drove through the back exit.

Benito utilized GPS to find an alternate route to the courthouse where the lab was housed, and Stefan relaxed. "Are you all right, Jane?"

Jane had scooted to the opposite side of the seat as if she feared he had some disease he might give her. He did not know whether to laugh or throttle her.

"Yes." She jerked her head to look out the window and remained stoic until they arrived at the lab. Benito parked behind the courthouse, and opened the door for Stefan. He climbed out then extended his hand to Jane. She studied it for a minute as if she intended to refuse, and he sighed.

"Come on, Jane, I do not have leprosy," he said, his patience strained. "Let us hurry inside before the mob at the hotel discovers we left and someone tracks us down."

A strand of hair fell across her face, and she swiped it back, then accepted his hand and crawled from the limo. Benito stepped to the side, hand at his gun, scanning the perimeter.

Suddenly a gunshot rang in the air. Jane startled, and Stefan grabbed her arm. "Get down!" he yelled.

She tried to jerk free, but he dragged her toward the door just as another gunshot ripped by her head.

Chapter Seven

"Stefan, get inside!" Jane shouted.

Stefan pushed her toward the entrance. "You first."

Another bullet pinged off the concrete wall, and Jane scanned the streets and spotted a dark sedan in the alley. The shooter was hiding behind it, firing at them.

She quickly searched for Benito. No, God... Stefan's guard was on the ground. Blood trickled from his chest.

She quickly retrieved her weapon, then shoved Stefan behind a streetlamp for cover. "Go inside now. I'll cover you!"

"No, I have to save Benito." Stefan lunged off the curb toward his security guard, but Jane caught his arm.

"Not until the shooter is caught," Jane cried. "Go inside now and call 9-1-1."

Another bullet zoomed near her head, and

Stefan threw himself on top of her, knocking her to the ground.

"Dammit, Stefan, what the hell are you doing?"

"Saving your life," he shouted.

Jane wiggled, trying to move. But Stefan was heavy and breathing hard, pinning her down. Footsteps clattered across the cement. She glanced to the side and spotted the shooter ducking behind a van.

"Move off of me so I can do my job." Jane gave him a hard shove, then rolled, jumped to her knees and fired at the shooter. The bullet pinged off the van, and the shooter darted into the alley on the opposite side of the courthouse.

A security guard from the lab rushed to the door, weapon drawn.

"Take the prince inside," Jane ordered. "And call 9-1-1!"

Stefan vaulted up to stop her from going after the shooter, but Jane took off running. Stefan's furious protests and pleas for her not to give chase echoed behind her as she disappeared into the alley.

Holding her weapon with a white-knuckled grip, she ducked as another bullet pinged toward her. Squinting through the shadows, she tried to look at the shooter, but his face was in the shadows. He was a burly guy though, clad in a dark leather jacket and black jeans.

Adrenaline pumping, she jogged around the back of the courthouse, then followed him past the local inn, the Boot 'n' Scoot shop and the diner, then he veered toward an abandoned warehouse.

She halted at the corner, searching all directions but saw nothing. Dammit. She'd lost him.

Pivoting again, her senses were honed as she inched her way along the side of the building. The scent of leather, saddle soap and machine oil wafted from the building. Scanning the dark interior, she slipped inside, poised for an attack.

A screech sounded and she jerked around but a piece of hard metal slammed her across the shoulder. She cried out, body slumping, then heard footsteps pounding the concrete flooring. Furious he'd gotten the drop on her, she fired her gun, but the man returned fire. She swung sideways, throwing herself against the wall, but the bullet grazed her cheek, stunning her.

Dizzy and disoriented, she grappled for control, a side door screeched open, and the shooter disappeared. A second later, the sound of a car engine burst to life, and she cursed.

Dammit, the bastard was getting away.

Staggering forward, she made her way to the door and raced outside, but the driver revved the motor, accelerating, and the vehicle careened from the parking lot. She ran after the car, determined to note the license plate, but the tag was missing.

This guy was a professional.

Blood trickled down her cheek as she strode back to the courthouse and she swiped it with her hand, her stomach knotting when she spotted Benito lying in a puddle of blood against the curb.

Praying he was still alive, she knelt and checked his pulse, but there was nothing.

STEFAN PACED INSIDE, enraged at the idea of standing behind closed doors guarded and safe while Jane chased after the man who'd tried to kill them. But the infuriating guard had called 9-1-1, then imprisoned him in some claustrophobic room the size of a coffin, and had perched himself in front of the door, arms crossed, body and weapon blocking Stefan from exiting the room.

"Ambulance and sheriff will be here momentarily," the security guard said.

"You cannot keep me captive. I need to check

on Jane." He stepped toward the door, but the guard threw up a hand, barring him from going any farther.

"I know Jane Cameron, Prince," the guard said in a deep voice. "She ordered me to keep you inside, and she'll have my head if I don't."

"She is not in charge," Stefan blurted. No woman had ever ordered him around. "Besides, my man was hit."

The guard cocked a brow but shook his bullylike head. "Sorry, sir. But she's the law, and if I were you, I wouldn't argue with her. Jane can be…" He hooked his thumbs in the belt of his pants. "What's the word for it? Bossy. Obstinate."

Stefan scrubbed his hand through his hair. "Impossible."

The guard grinned. "That, too."

"But what about my agent?" Stefan asked. "He needs me."

"I told you the ambulance is on its way along with the sheriff."

Outside, sirens wailed, confirming the guard's statement, footsteps sounded, and through the window, Stefan spotted blue lights swirling. He pictured Benito on the ground bleeding and dying, and his gut churned. Benito had saved his life.

And now he might have lost his own because of his loyalty.

Then an image of Jane injured, possibly dying herself, or trapped by the shooter while he did far worse, tormented him, and his pulse spiked.

He paced the room in a cold sweat. "I have to know if Jane is safe."

Static popped over the security guard's radio. He punched a button and Jane's voice echoed over the speaker.

"Wally, it's Jane. Is the prince all right?"

Stefan fisted his hands by his side.

"Yes, he's secured. Did you catch the shooter?"

"No, he got away. But the ambulance is here, and so is Sheriff Wolf."

"How can I help?" the guard asked.

"Just keep Prince Stefan secure while I process the crime scene."

"No," Stefan barked. "I wish to see Benito."

The guard leaned into the radio. "He's demanding to see his security agent."

A long heavy sigh followed, then Jane cleared her throat. "Tell him I'm sorry. But Benito didn't make it."

An icy coldness engulfed Stefan. He needed to get out of this room. Do something. He was a leader, a soldier, not some man to be treated as if he was a fragile piece of china. And not a man to be ordered around by an American female.

He jerked the radio from the guard and spoke into it himself. "Please, Jane," he said in a quiet but commanding voice. "Benito died protecting me. I must see him."

"Stefan…" Jane's voice cracked. "I know this is frustrating, but I'm just doing my job. Your safety is a priority. For all we know this shooter had an accomplice. He might be watching, ready to ambush you again."

"If it is so dangerous, then why are you out there in the open?" Stefan said, his voice rising with irritation.

"Because I'm a law enforcement officer, and I'm armed," Jane snapped.

"Then give me a weapon. I am an accomplished marksman."

"That's not the point," Jane said. "It's my job to protect you and process the crime scene."

"I do not need a woman's protection."

A tense moment passed. Stefan sensed he had crossed some line, but he did not care. He needed Jane out of harm's way.

"I don't have time to argue with you, Stefan. The police are here and we need to rope off the crime scene."

The sheriff's voice echoed in the background, then her superior's surly drawl.

"Please, Jane," Stefan said in a pleading tone that irked him because he had never pleaded with a woman before. "Let Osgood and Sheriff Wolf handle this while you come inside."

"I'll see you once I process the scene," Jane said curtly.

The static died, and the mic went silent. Blast! The infuriating woman had cut him off.

Before he kissed her again, he was going to shake some sense into her.

JANE RETRIEVED a crime scene kit, struggling with irritation over Stefan as Osgood took charge of roping off the crime scene. Didn't Stefan understand that he wasn't in Kyros anymore? That she was fully qualified to do her job, and that it was the twenty-first century? Women didn't have to kowtow to men in the U.S., and she was damn good at her job. Prince or not, she would never let him boss her around.

Sheriff Wolf approached Jane, his rugged face awash with concern as he scanned the scene. Behind him, the coroner Dr. Holstein followed, medical bag in hand. Danny Harold jumped from a news van, camera perched on his shoulder, and sauntered toward her.

Jane gave Osgood a jerk of the head, indicating the press had arrived, and he made a beeline for Harold. Good, let him deal with the jerk.

Sheriff Wolf crooked his thumb toward the bloody mess. "What happened?"

Jane lifted her camera to photograph the body. "Prince Stefan and I came to the lab so he could review some evidence."

Sheriff Wolf narrowed his eyes. "Why would you allow the prince to examine evidence?"

Jane sighed. "He's an expert in explosives, and I couldn't identify some of the particles from the bomb site."

Jane gestured across the street. "But when we approached the building, a man shot at us from over there."

The coroner dropped down beside Stefan's security agent and began examining the body.

"Can you describe the shooter?" Sheriff Wolf asked.

She shook her head, wiping at the perspiration on her neck. The summer heat was already kicking in, the temperature rising. "No. But he was big, burly, wore a black leather jacket and hat."

"Hmm, sounds like a hired gun."

"That's what I thought," Jane said. "The tag was missing on the car he escaped in as well."

Dr. Holstein glanced up over his bifocals. "Looks like one bullet hit the victim in the abdomen, but the other punctured his heart. He didn't last long."

"Where's the prince?" the sheriff asked.

"Inside." Jane snapped a photograph of the body from different angles. "One of our own guards secured him while I chased the shooter into the alley."

"Looks like you were hit," Dr. Holstein commented as he stood.

Jane rubbed a finger over her cheek. "Just grazed. It's no big deal."

Dr. Holstein stepped closer to examine her injury. "The medics are on their way. They can clean it up for you."

"After I process the scene." Jane glanced up at the sky where thunderclouds had gathered. "I want to finish before it rains and contaminates the evidence."

Sheriff Wolf turned and scrutinized the street and area surrounding the courthouse. "What about the make and model of the shooter's vehicle?"

"Some kind of dark sedan," Jane said. "Four doors."

Several onlookers had started to gather, gawking and asking questions.

"Let me canvas the area, see if anyone else saw or heard anything," the sheriff said.

Jane spotted a bullet casing. "Yep, let's get to work. We have a killer to catch, and if he is a pro, he'll be back."

Sheriff Wolf strode over to the spectators and reminded them to stay behind the crime tape. Jane saw Osgood arguing with Harold, so she focused on photographing the dead man and bullet casings she found. She studied the angles and trajectory, her and Stefan's location as they'd left the vehicle and walked to the courthouse, and searched the perimeter.

She found three casings from her own gun and bagged them, then five casings from the shooter. Shining her flashlight across the edge of the street near the dark sedan where the shooter had hidden, she located a partial footprint and took a cast of it to compare with ones from the bomb site.

Together she and Osgood searched the stretch between the courthouse and warehouse, then ran flashlights along the area looking for forensics.

"What did you tell Harold?" Jane asked as she snagged a loose fiber from a clump of weeds next to the building.

"The truth. An unidentified shooter fired at

you and Prince Stefan. Another unidentified man was killed."

Jane sighed. "He was working for Stefan," Jane said.

And Stefan was probably beating himself up over his death.

She rolled her shoulders, frustrated. Worse, they were still no closer to figuring out who was behind the bomb or to finding the sheik.

STEFAN PACED the small office teeming with anger. How dare Jane leave him behind closed doors, waiting, unaware of what was going on?

His cell phone buzzed, and he realized that his friends at the resort might have heard the news. With one finger he connected the call while he glanced through the window in search of Jane.

"Stefan, it's Efraim. We just saw the news. Are you all right?"

"Yes," Stefan said. "When Jane and I arrived at the crime lab, we were ambushed and Benito was shot. I am afraid he did not survive."

Efraim muttered a word of frustration. "Did you see the shooter?"

"From a distance," Stefan mumbled in frustration. "Jane chased him into an alley, and now I am being held in this claustrophobic room."

A heartbeat of silence stretched between them. "I understand it is difficult," Efraim said. "But we must remember the bigger picture and what is at stake. The summit, our country's futures."

Stefan pinched the bridge of his nose. "I am aware of that. But I cannot tolerate Jane being in danger while I sit and do nothing."

"We're all feeling antsy here," Efraim said, his voice strained. "We are men of action, leaders, commanders."

"Exactly. Speak to Fahad, see if he is making any headway with those lists."

"Yes, of course."

Sheriff Wolf walked past the glass window to the door, then pushed it open.

"I have to go, Efraim," Stefan said. "The sheriff is here. I shall keep you informed." He disconnected, then turned to the sheriff, anxious.

"I'm sorry about your security agent," Sheriff Wolf said. "The coroner will have him transported to the morgue. If you'll let us know who to call, we'll inform his family."

Stefan swallowed against the guilt clogging his throat. "Certainly. Where is Jane?"

"The paramedics are taking care of her now," the sheriff said. "She'll be inside in a few minutes."

Stefan staggered backward as if he'd been punched. "Paramedics? Then she was shot?"

Sheriff Wolf studied him with hooded eyes. "It's only a flesh wound. Now tell me your version of what happened out there."

An image of Jane bleeding ripped through his head, and Stefan fisted his hands by his sides. Benito killed and Jane hurt?

While he stood safely tucked inside.

It was preposterous. An injustice. A blasted disgrace!

"Prince?" Sheriff Wolf said. "Did you see the shooter or his getaway car?"

"I did not see the car," Stefan said through clenched teeth. "But I did catch a glimpse of the man. He was tall, over six feet, hefty. And he wore a black leather bomber jacket and hat."

Sheriff Wolf tapped his notepad. "That's what Jane said. Anything else?"

Stefan glanced at the door desperate to see Jane, the past hour haunting him. "He had thick eyebrows, and a scar on his chin."

"Good."

The door swung open, and Jane finally appeared, her clothes slightly disheveled, her hair a mess as if she'd run her hands through it a dozen times. His gaze roved over her, hungry, angry, terrified at the thought that she might have been killed because of him.

Then his gaze zeroed in on her left cheek, and pure rage flooded him. A bullet had grazed her skin, leaving it red and raw as if it had burned the flesh, and her jaw was already swelling.

"You should be in the hospital," he said, tension making his words sound harsh.

"It's not a big deal." She met his gaze. "It's just a flesh wound, Stefan."

"It looks nasty," he snapped. "Were you injured anywhere else?"

She shook her head but averted her eyes, rousing his suspicions. "Jane, do not lie. Where are you hurt?"

"I'm not," she said, her eyes spewing a warning. "Just furious that the bastard got away."

Normally he might flinch at her language, but he felt like cursing himself, something a prince rarely did. But being shot at, watching a man die to save him, and knowing a woman had been hurt in the process of protecting him, were enough to destroy any semblance he had of manners.

Right now he was just a man who was beginning to care about this hardheaded, gun-carrying woman.

She indicated the metal box in her hand.

"Now, the sooner I process this evidence, the sooner we might be able to determine who our shooter is."

Through the glass window of the office, Stefan saw two medics carrying a body in a black nylon bag and his stomach twisted. Benito.

Jane angled her head toward Stefan. "I heard that you requested to see Benito. The morgue is downstairs," Jane said. "The sheriff and our guard can escort you."

Stefan studied her bruised face, the firm set of her delicate jaw, the determination in her eyes and knew Jane was upset over losing his security agent, that somehow she saw it as a personal failure.

"Thank you," he said quietly. "I would like that. But I do not wish for you to be alone unprotected."

Jane sighed. "The shooter was after you, Stefan, not me."

Stefan caught her arm. "But he might use you to get to me," he said in a low voice. "And I will not allow that to happen."

He itched to lift his hand and touch her cheek, to drag her into his arms and make sure she was all right. He needed to feel her against him. To hold her and touch his lips to hers and taste that she was still alive.

But the sheriff was present, so he restrained himself.

"Go say goodbye to Benito," Jane said softly. "Then I want you to examine those bomb particles."

Stefan nodded. The sooner they determined who the shooter was and who was behind the bombing, the sooner they could end this fiasco and everyone would be safe.

Including Jane.

He would die himself before he let anyone hurt her.

Chapter Eight

Jane felt the anger radiating from Stefan like a hot poker and wanted to extinguish it. But she had a job to do, and he needed to understand that her job meant everything to her.

She didn't have time to worry about his macho pride, which had to be the reason for his strong reaction. It wasn't as if he actually cared about *her*.

He was just feeling guilty over his security agent's death and frustrated that they hadn't caught the person behind the attacks. If the shooter was even the same person who'd orchestrated the explosion.

For all they knew, they could be unrelated, or both incidents masterminded by some group of terrorists.

Determined to do her part in finding the answers, she carried her evidence box into the crime lab. Stefan followed.

"Where is that irritating Mr. Osgood?" Stefan asked in a gruff voice.

"Checking security cameras outside. Maybe the camera captured a picture of the shooter or his getaway vehicle."

Sheriff Wolf poked his head inside the door. "Would you like to see your friend now?"

Stefan glanced at Jane. "You will be safe here?"

Jane patted her weapon. "Yes. Now go. By the time you return, I might have some information on the shooter's weapon." She'd also found a few drops of blood beside the warehouse that could have belonged to the shooter, and partial prints on one of the bullet casings.

Maybe she'd injured the bastard and he would have to seek medical help.

Stefan stared at her for another long minute, the tension palpable, then finally exited, and followed the sheriff down the hall.

Adrenaline had been churning through Jane, but she felt the first strains of it waning, and leaned against the counter with her head in her hands. Dear God, it had been close out there.

Stefan could have been killed in a second.

Forcing deep pockets of air into her lungs to calm herself, she counted to ten. *Focus on work. Do the job.*

Forget about how startling and intense Stefan's eyes are. About how your heart had jumped to your throat when you thought he might be hit.

You can't allow this case to become personal. And you can't fall for Prince Stefan Lutece.

Her resolve tacked into place, she lifted her head and went to work. She asked Tomas to check local hospitals and emergency clinics in case she had seriously injured the shooter. God, she hoped she had.

With gloved hands, she dug the bullet casings she'd collected from the envelope she'd stored them in, then began to analyze them.

Tomas retrieved the clothes of the victim to analyze the blood splatter. Jane had studied the scene enough to determine that there was only one shooter.

Now for more details of the bullet. Each firearm's interior barrels were rifled or grooved in order to make the bullet spin and increase its accuracy. She examined the markings of each casing she'd found, a process called ballistic fingerprinting, and digitally ran them through ATF's National Integrated Ballistic Information Network. She not only needed to determine the type of weapon, but also wanted to see if this shooter's weapon had been used in any other crimes.

She let the computer program do its work, and waited while it ran comparisons, then frowned when the make and model of the gun appeared on the screen.

A Russian handgun. This model was constructed for hitting armored targets—second or third class protective vests and vehicles. At 100 meters range, it could pierce thirty layers of Kevlar or 2.8 titanium plate.

Russian Special Forces used it as a special sniper weapon.

She pushed back her chair, contemplating what she'd learned. If a sniper used this gun, he could be current or former Special Forces.

Confirming this was a professional job.

Someone had taken out a hit on Stefan, which meant that they wouldn't stop until the job was finished.

STEFAN PRESSED a hand to Benito's shoulder, his heart heavy. Benito had been a faithful employee, and although he'd never met his family, the man had a wife back home in Kyros. He phoned Edilio and requested he inform the family of the tragic news.

He would compensate the man's wife financially, of course, but money did not bring back a loved one.

His thoughts turned to Jane as he ended the call, and for some insane reason, his heart swelled with longing. He wanted to see her again. He hated to leave her alone for even a moment lest whoever was trying to assassinate him returned. Was the shooter the same person who had caused the explosion?

Did he have Amir? If so, why would he not contact them with demands?

Fearing the worst, that the absence of a call indicated that Amir might already be dead, he struggled for calm. So many people were opposed to the summit, yet he and his friends knew that their compact could not only save their small nations but also aid the U.S.

He could not give up or retreat now.

"Thank you, Dr. Holstein," Stefan said. "I am most grateful for the respect and care you gave my friend."

Dr. Holstein adjusted his glasses. "I hope the police find out who did this, Prince Stefan. I've heard good things about what your compact is offering, and I pray the remainder of your trip is more peaceful."

He hoped so, too.

He excused himself, then allowed the guard

to escort him to the elevator, then down the corridor to the lab.

The guard opened the door and Stefan stepped inside, suddenly aware that his heart was beating more rapidly, that his palms felt sweaty as if he was some awkward teenager approaching the girl he had a crush on.

Except this girl carried a weapon, was bossy and independent, and had been injured saving his life.

"The bullet casings came from a Russian sniper gun," Jane said without preamble. "It was a professional hit, Stefan."

Stefan was not surprised. "Any number of my enemies, or Amir's, could have Russian connections."

Jane nodded. "I also found a few blood droplets that don't belong to Benito. I ran them, but they didn't show up in the system." She paused. "I can't be certain they belonged to the shooter, but if we catch him, we can compare, and it might help in court."

"I see."

"I can also ask the FBI to explore international databases," Jane offered. "I have a friend, Special Agent Frank Priebus, who I trust. He could help us."

"Let me discuss it with Fahad. He has his own sources which we would prefer."

Jane folded her arms. "Still don't want the attacks public, do you?"

"Absolutely not."

She motioned for him to follow her to a microscope and computer. "Here are those particles you wanted to examine."

She gestured toward the microscope, and he looked into the lens. Then he scanned the results on her computer screen. Worry tightened his jaw as he analyzed the data.

"What do you think?" Jane asked.

"It is as I feared when I saw your report." He lifted his gaze to hers. "A new type of bomb material that is being experimented with," he said, watching his language carefully.

"You mean in the Middle East?"

He gave a clipped nod.

"Does it have to do with nuclear weapons?"

"There are possibilities," he said quietly. "But it is in early stages. And in this small amount, not lethal as far as being biochemically hazardous."

"Damn." The coloring fled from her face. "So we're dealing with a Russian sniper and possibly a military connection involved in biochemical warfare?"

Stefan hated the fear and disgust on her face. This turn of events made matters tenfold worse. It would feed those who believed the COIN members were here on a fishing expedition for knowledge of just such weapons.

"I am sorry, Jane," he said, his throat thick. "My friends and I came here on a mission of peace and goodwill. And now..." Benito's ghostly face flashed in his head. "And now, look what has happened..."

Stefan wanted to say more, but Osgood suddenly appeared in the doorway, so he ceased speaking. Although he might agree with the man that Jane should not be working this dangerous job, he would not pretend to like him.

After all, he understood the male psyche. Osgood might criticize her and be a bully, but from the way the man's eyes roved over her as he entered the room and the jealousy that had tinged his voice when he'd found Stefan embracing her, he realized the imbecile's attitude toward Jane was his own clumsy way of flirting with her. The man wanted in her pants, as the Americans would say.

And as long as he was here, alive and with a breath left in his chest, the man would not put his hands on Jane. No one would.

Except him, of course.

JANE STARED up at Osgood, irritated for the intrusion although she had no idea why. She and Stefan certainly weren't engaged in anything personal at the moment.

But the agony in Stefan's eyes when he'd spoken about Benito made her heart clench, and for a brief second, she'd been tempted to comfort him.

"Did you find anything?" Osgood asked bluntly.

Jane indicated the ballistics report and explained her findings. "Prince Stefan also identified the suspicious bomb particles as a new type of material that has the potential for use in biochemical warfare."

Osgood gave Stefan a suspicious look, and Jane blew out a breath. "How about you? Anything on the security tapes or any witnesses?"

He shook his head. "This guy knew what he was doing. He shot out the outside cameras facing the car where he was hiding, and the one in the alley."

"And the warehouse?

"Cameras aren't working. The owner had some financial trouble and security was first to go."

"Great." Jane sighed then crooked a thumb

toward Stefan. "I'm going with him back to the resort to pick up my SUV."

Stefan stiffened, and Jane braced herself for another argument. "I can call a driver and arrange for your vehicle to be brought to you."

"That's not necessary. I can drive the limo," Jane said, jutting up her chin defiantly. "Unless you don't trust me to protect you."

Stefan's nostrils flared with anger, making a small smile tilt her mouth. She knew it was a challenge, and she wanted to see how he would handle it.

"Of course I trust you, Miss CSI Jane Cameron," he said tersely. "You have already proven your willingness to mindlessly throw yourself in front of harm's way for your job."

It was for you, you buffoon, she thought silently, then realized the mistake in that thinking. Truth was, she'd never had to draw her weapon before. Most of her work had taken place at the lab, not in combat.

But she would do it again in a heartbeat if it meant keeping him from getting killed.

"Just doing what I can for the bigwigs," she said sarcastically.

His brows puckered together, and she realized he might not understand her sarcasm, but simply shrugged. "Come on, let's go."

Amazingly, Stefan followed her without comment. But she felt the anger simmering below the surface as she asked the guard to escort them to the limo. The police had cordoned off the front of the courthouse and alley, and another guard stood out front for precaution.

Stefan slid into the passenger seat of the limo, snapped his seat belt, then stared out the window at the police SUV still parked on the curb. Her own gaze found the blood-splattered pavement where Benito had lain, and she realized that Stefan's eyes were glued to that spot. That Stefan didn't value one life over another, that even though he had no choice but to accept protection because of his position, guilt plagued him now for his man's death.

Sympathy and compassion rolled through her, and she couldn't resist. She slipped her hand over his and squeezed it. A muscle ticked in his strong jaw, but he didn't look at her. He simply curled his hand below hers, and held it tightly as if having that human touch meant something important to him.

As if she did.

But that idea was ludicrous.

Still, for a moment, like a fool, she allowed herself to imagine that it was true. That a handsome prince actually could be attracted to a plain Jane like her.

HUMILIATION WASHED over Stefan at the mere idea that Jane was his protector. He was the man. The military hero. The leader of his country.

He did not want her taking care of him.

Her fingers stroked his and something warm and strange rippled through him. No, he didn't want Jane taking care of him—except perhaps in the bedroom.

And there he yearned to take care of her as well.

She parked at the resort, and he beeped his security team to meet them. He refused to gamble with Jane's life.

Jane remained on edge, alert, as Edilio appeared with two guards, and the group surrounded them as they entered. Stefan headed straight to the conference room where Efraim had gathered with Sebastian and Antoine.

Efraim's brows pinched together as he spotted Jane. "I thought we agreed to be careful who we trusted."

Stefan squared his shoulders. "We do. But Miss Cameron and I have an agreement, and I believe we can depend on her."

"Is it true?" Sebastian asked. "A sniper tried to kill you?"

"Yes," Stefan said. "Outside the courthouse."

A rumble of concern ripped through the room. "Do you have any idea who he was or who sent him?" Antoine asked.

Stefan gestured toward Jane, and she cleared her throat, then explained about the Russian sniper weapon and the blood at the scene. "Sheriff Wolf is checking local hospitals and emergency clinics in case I injured the perpetrator."

Stefan directed his comment to Fahad. "I need you to contact your sources for Russian connections. We could be dealing with a Russian mob or gang who is opposed to our summit or one who hires themselves out as assassins."

"Yes, sir," Fahad said. "I have agents checking into the lists each of you gave me as well as the sheik's personal enemies."

Efraim wrung his hands together. "I cannot stand sitting by and doing nothing while our friend may be held as hostage or worse. He may be enduring torture."

"Stay calm," Fahad said. "We have experienced agents investigating the matter. Do not make it more difficult by exposing yourselves to our enemies."

Murmurs of frustration, discontent and protests followed.

"He's right," Jane said. "Let the police do their jobs. Meanwhile, you can make it easier if you remain secure at the resort."

Stefan knew she was right, but he didn't like it. The others parted, still grumbling that they were antsy and needed to do something. Stefan did not trust the locals, but he did trust Jane, and he wanted to tie her down and keep her secure in his bedchamber.

There she would be safe.

And pleasured.

"I'll escort you to your quarters," Jane said.

Anticipation streaked through Stefan, but Jane's look did not indicate that she entertained sexual fantasies about him. Blast it.

"Then I'm going to return to the lab," Jane continued, oblivious to his lustful fantasies. "Maybe Osgood or Tomas found something on the other forensics I brought in from the shooting site."

Stefan agreed, but only because he wanted to get her alone. He motioned for one of the guards to follow them, then escorted her through a back corridor, then outside through the private garden to his own suite of rooms.

"You mentioned a list," Jane said. "Is there

anyone who sticks out to you? Someone with Russian ties?"

Stefan strode to his computer, hit print and waited until the list spilled from the printer. "It is possible." Jarryd in particular. "Edilio is investigating them now."

"Good," Jane said. "I hope you'll let me know if we need to alert our local police."

"Of course." Stefan flexed his sweating hands. "I insist you extract yourself from this investigation, Jane."

Jane's startled gaze swung to his. "What?"

"You heard me," he said in his most authoritarian voice, the one that evoked obedience from his staff and the military forces he had commanded. "I wish you off the case immediately."

"Why?" Jane asked, her voice on edge. "I thought you trusted me. I agreed to keep your concerns about the sheik confidential, and I've kept my word."

"It is not that," Stefan said, his gaze zeroing in on her bruised cheek. "This situation is too dangerous."

Jane's face burned with anger. "Stefan, I understand you've had a rough day, but my career means everything to me. As long as you're here on U.S. soil, I will do that job and protect you.

And I'll do my best to try to find out who tried to kill you."

Stefan wondered why her job was so important. Simply looking at that red flesh wound on her cheek infuriated him. "Your work is more important than your life?" he asked in a low voice.

"My work *is* my life," Jane said matter-of-factly.

Unable to resist, he reached up and gently traced a finger along her injured jaw. "Why is that? Why are people not more important? Why are sunsets and long lazy rides on horseback and fine dinners not part of your life as well?"

"People are important," Jane said with conviction. "That's why I do what I do. I want to get justice for those who've been wronged. But I don't have time for long lazy rides or fine dinners." Not that she'd had any recent invitations.

"You should, Jane. You deserve such pleasures." He angled his head so he could see into her eyes. "Or does getting close to someone frighten you more than dying?"

Her eyes flared with discomfort, and he sensed he had guessed correctly. Someone had hurt her before.

He did not intend to let that happen again.

"Who made you run from men, Jane?"

"Stefan," Jane whispered hoarsely.

"Who?" he asked, wishing he could rip off their limbs one by one for daring to hurt such a lovely creature.

She closed her eyes for a moment as if she did not plan to answer, and when she opened them, such a deep vulnerability registered in her eyes that his chest clenched.

"I don't have to run from men," Jane said. "They aren't chasing me, Stefan. In case you haven't noticed, I'm not exactly a beauty queen."

Shock bolted through Stefan. "Then the American men are blind idiots."

Her breath quickened at his compliment, and heat darkened her eyes, the kind of heat that made a man's body harden.

The kind that made his heart swell with longing. "Now, you must excuse yourself from this case." He traced his finger lower, then over her lips. Lips that were soft and delicate and made him yearn for another taste.

He had promised he would not kiss her at work. That the next time it would be a proper kiss.

"Stefan, please," she whispered.

Her throaty voice washed over him, igniting

the fire in his body. "Please, what? Please kiss you…"

His heart fluttered like a schoolboy's as her lips puckered beneath his fingers.

Then she glanced at the signet ring he wore, the one emboldened with an etching of the crown, and started to pull away. "Please let me get back to work."

He shook his head. "No, I could not live with myself if such a lovely, intelligent, sexy woman like you lost her life because of me."

She shook her head in denial. "You don't need to compliment me, Stefan."

He tilted her chin up with his thumb, forcing her to see the raw need in his own eyes. He wanted her to feel the same intense heat that consumed him.

He wanted her to want him the way he wanted her.

So he made good on his promise. He lowered his head, closed his mouth over hers, and kissed her with every ounce of his being.

A proper kiss. Only there was nothing proper about it at all.

Chapter Nine

Jane's pulse clamored as Stefan closed his lips over hers. His lips felt soft and gentle yet at the same time, hard and demanding, as if he expected her to kiss him back.

And how could she possibly resist? His concern for her safety touched her deeply. He wasn't just a handsome, charismatic leader. He was intelligent, caring, a man who'd fought for his country in the military, a man who had great pride and character.

A man who said he couldn't live with himself if she died.

A man with muscles that were rippling beneath her body as she pressed her chest against his. A man who could have any woman in the world he wanted, but for some reason she couldn't fathom, he seemed to want her.

At least for the moment.

And this moment was all that mattered.

They had been shot at earlier, and both of

them could have been killed. She needed this. Needed to feel his arms around her, his lips on hers, his body hot and heavy against her own.

He deepened the kiss, probing her lips apart with his tongue and teasing the warm cavern of her mouth with erotic tongue lashes. She met him thrust for thrust, sigh for sigh, groan for groan.

A throaty moan of pleasure and need ripped from him, and he cupped her face with his hands, sinking deeper into the kiss, so deeply that she thought he might swallow her.

As if he was branding her as his.

The feeling overwhelmed her, frightened her, made her feel like…giving herself to him completely.

His hands trailed down her shoulders, to her waist, then he cupped her bottom and pulled her to him. Warmth spread through her, stark and needy, and she moaned as she felt his thick erection pulsing against her thigh.

Dear heavens. He did want her.

Her legs buckled slightly, and he caught her, trailing kisses down her throat and neck, loving her with his tongue and nibbling at the sensitive spot behind her ear. She clung to his shoulders, heaving for a breath and trying to control her heartbeat, which felt as if it was going to burst out of her chest.

His mouth traced a path downward, and he made soft suckling sounds as he kissed the swell of her breasts. One hand pushed her T-shirt up, and she ran her fingers through his hair, clawing at him wildly.

Passion exploded between them as he placed his lips on her breasts, teasing at the lace of her bra and catching the top with his teeth to drag it downward, exposing one ripe nipple.

She arched against him, practically purring and silently begging him to take that nipple between his lips. He obeyed as if he understood her needs, as if he craved her body as much as she craved his.

Pure pleasure coursed through her as his mouth consumed her, and she pushed at his jacket, wanting his clothes off, her clothes off, to be totally naked with him.

He tossed his jacket to the chair, then lifted her shirt over her head, exposing her lace-clad breasts. A moment of insecurity assaulted her, and she started to cover herself, but he grabbed her hands and pushed them down beside her, holding them while he looked his fill.

"You are exquisite, Jane Cameron," he

said thickly. "More beautiful than I have imagined."

Surprise flared inside her. "You imagined me like this?"

"From the very first moment I saw you." A sultry smile tilted his full lips, making him look impossibly sexy and rakish. He began to unbutton his own shirt. "Do not tell me that you have not pictured us together—" he gestured toward their harried state of undress "—like this." He lowered his head and leaned into her ear. "Naked. Together. Making love."

Jane's breath caught. Never had a man made love to her with his eyes. Touched her with his mouth as if he could lap her up like sweet cream.

Spoken to her in such a bold sexy way.

Made her want to strip and throw him down and have her way with him.

And let him do anything he wanted with her.

The thought scared the bejeezus out of her.

She took a step backward, but he yanked her up against him. "Do not run, Jane. I know you feel the heat between us just as I do."

She did feel it. And she wanted him. Even if just for the night.

Succumbing to her desires was not something

plain Jane usually did, but this time was different. This time she reached for him, brushed her fingers against his bare chest, caught the heady scent of his need in the breath he exhaled at her touch.

Tonight she was going to do something she never did. She was going to fall into his arms and savor every second.

SUDDENLY a knock sounded at the door. "Prince Stefan, it's Hector. I must speak with you."

Stefan stilled, then pulled Jane behind him. "Come back later, Hector."

"But, sir, it is important. I've spoken with your father."

Stefan dropped his head forward with a low groan. "Forgive me, Jane. But my father has been ill. I must take this."

Behind him, Jane's labored sigh filled the air. Tremulous, husky, laced with unspent passion and disappointment.

All the emotions he felt.

Then the rustling of clothes.

Hector knocked again. "Prince—"

"One moment, Hector."

He spun around, an apology on his lips as well as a promise to finish what they'd begun once he had conferred with Hector, but Jane's expression stopped him cold.

She looked mortified, harried, full of regret.

Had he pushed too hard? Hadn't Jane wanted him?

Insecurity cut through him.

"I am sorry, Jane."

Anger underscored her gaze, followed by a moment of hurt. "You are?"

"I do not want to hurt you." His throat was so thick he had to swallow twice. "I—"

"Stefan!" Hector shouted.

Blast it! He never cursed in front of a lady and he refused to now. But he had the oddest feeling he'd just made a mistake with Jane. Trouble was, he wasn't sure how or what that mistake was.

He still wanted her with a fever that was lighting his body up like a match to dry wood. Jane hastily pulled her T-shirt over her head and straightened her clothing, and he did the same while he contemplated how to proceed.

Perhaps he should have asked her to wait in his bedroom.

But Jane's expression was closed as if the opportunity was lost forever.

"I'll step outside while you speak with your chief aide," Jane said, her professional demeanor tacked into place.

"Do not leave, Jane," Stefan said in a low voice. "We are not finished."

She reached for the door, her gaze still simmering with unleashed passion and something else. A wariness that troubled him more than he dared admit.

"Yes, we still have a case to solve," Jane said matter-of-factly. "Now I should get back to work."

Her statement sounded final, as if she was declaring war against any further intimacy, but this was one war he intended to win. Miss Jane Cameron was going to be his.

With a stubborn hilt to her body, she opened the door. Hector stood facing her, but she moved past him without turning back. Stefan felt the distance between them as if that door had not only physically erected a wall between them, but as if it had emotionally as well.

He itched to go after her, but Hector's craggy face was drawn with worry and sorrow.

"Hector, what is wrong? Has something happened to Father?"

Hector sighed wearily. "He is frail, Prince. Frail and demanding to know what is happening here."

Stefan scrubbed his hand over his face. "I hope you did not tell him."

"No," Hector said. "But we cannot keep the news from him forever. Not with Benito's death…"

Stefan felt the weight on his shoulders. "Yes, I know."

"Prince Stefan, I am so sorry to hear that Benito was killed." Hector's gray eyes filled with grief. "Thankfully, you were not hit."

Stefan made a sound of disgust. "Thanks to Miss Cameron, who shoved me inside."

Hector's brows lifted at Stefan's derisive tone. "Then we should thank Miss Cameron."

Anger tightened Stefan's shoulder blades. "Yes, but I do not like other's lives jeopardized to save mine. Poor Benito…his family." Anguish for them made his chest ache.

Hector poured Stefan a scotch straight up and handed it to him. "Do not blame yourself, Your Highness. Benito understood the risks and joined your team because he believed in you and your policies."

"Which leaves me to figure out who did not," Stefan said, his anger mounting.

Hector shifted, walked to the window and looked out as if he were searching for potential enemies, then turned to him with an odd expression on his face. "I understand that you received a warning not to trust anyone here," Hector began.

Stefan tossed down the scotch. "Yes. But we still do not know the source."

"Are you certain you can trust Miss Cameron?"

Stefan set the glass down with a thud. "She has given me no reason not to trust her."

"But she is—how do the Americans say?— cozying up to you?"

Stefan scoffed. "Hardly." It was more like he was chasing her and she was running as fast as humanly possible. "Why? Have you been spying on me, Hector?"

Hector's face paled, guilt claiming his eyes. "I would not use the term spying, sir. But I am, as always, looking out for your best interests."

"I am a grown man, Hector. I can take care of my own interests."

"But you are vulnerable now. And this Jane woman, she does not fit into your station in life. Into your future."

Ire rose within Stefan. Hector rarely interfered with his personal life. "Hector, I do not wish to discuss Jane with you."

Hector held up an arthritic hand. "I understand, sir. And I respect your wishes, but you and your friends are in danger. And there are things you should know about Miss Cameron."

Stefan gritted his teeth. Did Jane have some deep dark secrets? A shaded past?

He could not imagine.

And he did not want to ask. Somehow doing so felt like a violation.

But Hector was correct. If he had information that affected his friends, he had to know. He owed it to Benito not to bury his head in the sand. "What are you saying, Hector?"

"That you should not become personally involved with her," Hector said. "You have your country to consider, and if this compact is not signed as you planned, you must obey your father's wishes and marry Princess Daria."

Daria? He could not believe his ears. "Hector, you are out of line here."

"I'm sorry, Prince. But I have been your father's adviser for years, and I am only looking out for both of you now. And for Kyros."

"My relationship with Jane has nothing to do with Kyros."

Hector shrugged, but his gaze penetrated Stefan. "Unfortunately you know that any woman you choose to be with can impact your future as Kyros' leader."

Hector's words grated on Stefan, although he could not deny there was truth to the words.

"Even Daria's brother Butrus is not in favor of the marriage."

"That may be true. But he has his own motives."

Stefan poured himself another drink.

Would Butrus have him killed to stop the marriage? He would ask Edilio to discreetly find out.

Hector folded his hands and cleared his throat. "Are you aware that Jane Cameron does not know who her father is? That her mother was a beautiful woman who chased the limelight, chased dignitaries. That she committed suicide after her husband cheated on her?" Hector paused and removed a news article clipping from his pocket and laid it on the bar. "The gossip surrounding the affair and her mother's death placed Miss Cameron into the media when she was a child."

Stefan's heart squeezed as he studied the photo of Jane at the age of twelve. A tall, gangly, slightly awkward Jane who had not yet come into womanhood.

Then the photograph of her mother who looked glamorous standing beside a French ambassador. A woman who obviously had stars in her eyes and loved the attention. In that photo Jane was standing off to the side, looking stricken as if her mother had purposely banned her from the camera. As if she'd been embarrassed that Jane was not all glitz and glamour.

"Perhaps she is like her mother," Hector said. "Perhaps she has aspirations of marrying a prince and living in the limelight herself now."

"No," Stefan said, unable to fathom Jane being manipulative. If anything, Jane seemed to avoid attention to herself.

But now he understood her hesitation regarding him in the beginning.

"What happened to Jane after her mother's death?" Stefan asked.

"She went to live with an aunt and uncle. The uncle was a police officer."

That experience probably inspired her to become a criminologist herself.

Hector sighed. "The point I'm making is that this police officer woman has no place beside you as you assume full leadership of Kyros. What would your people think?"

"And Daria would be the perfect bride?" Stefan asked bitterly.

"Yes." Hector did not mince words. "Again, sir, I must remind you of your mission. You are scheduled to visit and tour one of the local oil drilling sites. Do you still intend to examine the facilities and hold the press conference on site to point out the environmental problems and your plans to alleviate them?"

Stefan hated the reminder of Daria and his status. But he had been too busy dodging danger and trying to find out what happened to Amir to focus on his original plan.

But not following through with the summit meant that he was allowing whoever was terrorizing him and his friends, whoever was trying to stop the COIN compact, to win.

And Stefan would not allow defeat. If Amir had been kidnapped or was dead, they would carry on in honor of their friend.

Daria's face flashed in his mind, followed by Jane's, and he gritted his teeth. He wanted Jane more and more each time he saw her. Her strength and vulnerability stirred his admiration just as her body and lips stirred his passion.

As for Daria—he did not love her, but Hector was correct. Marrying her would make his father happy and save their country.

Being the leader of a country sometimes required personal sacrifice.

If the compact did not work, he would be forced to do his duty and take King Nazim's daughter as his wife.

Chapter Ten

Jane breathed in the fresh night air as she paced the gardens outside Stefan's suite. The scent of flowers, mesquite and grass filled the air, the brilliant colors of the Indian paintbrush, canna lilies, foxglove, poppies and coneflowers dotting the landscape as their petals danced in the evening breeze.

Separated by gardens, crisp green lawns with walking trails and gurgling streams, the private quarters were both luxurious and rustic and a perfect haven for the prince and sheiks.

Except that now murder tainted their trip, a murder she needed to solve to ensure Stefan's safety.

Dammit. In spite of her resolve not to become involved with him, she cared more about his safety than she wanted to admit.

She also wanted to go back in his suite and get gloriously naked with him.

Frustrated with herself, she slumped onto

the garden bench and stared into the bubbling fountain.

Thank goodness Stefan's chief aide had interrupted or she would be making love with him right now.

And that would be a huge mistake.

Jane Cameron was a working girl. A plain girl. A girl who did not give her body away easily.

Or her heart.

And unlike some of the modern girls she knew, her body and heart were tied together in one complicated knot.

How had she let this happen? How could she be so foolish?

She stood, knowing she needed to leave. She could not go back inside and see Stefan tonight or breathe his intoxicating scent, not while her heart sat on her sleeve ready for him to pillage it.

From her vantage point in the garden, she heard voices and Stefan's door opened. He stood for a moment talking to his chief aide, then the older man disappeared toward the neighboring guesthouse. Jane expected Stefan to retreat back inside to rest, but instead he exited his cottage and headed up the path.

He was alone. No security guard.

She stepped from the canopy of flowers into his path. "Where are you going, Stefan?"

He halted abruptly, his eyes widening at the sight of her. "I...thought you had left, Jane."

Hunger spiraled in her belly as his gaze moved over her. Desperate to fight temptation, she resorted to taking the offensive. "I...no." She folded her arms. "You shouldn't be out here alone. Where are your guards?"

Agitation lined his face. "I needed some space, time to think."

Did he mean from her as well?

"But it's not safe for you, Stefan."

"A man cannot always play by the rules." A sliver of something sexual possessed his eyes then, and he reached up and tucked an unruly strand of her hair behind one ear. "Perhaps I like a little bit of danger."

She trembled inside. Maybe he did. But she didn't. At least not with her heart.

"Please, Stefan, go back inside. Let your security team protect you so you can finish your business in the States."

Her words seemed to tame the suggestive look in his eyes. She missed it. But she also knew it was for the best.

"That is the reason I came out," he admitted. "Hector reminded me that giving in to the threat, allowing whoever is terrorizing us to prevent the summit, is wrong. It gives our enemies power."

Jane studied his demeanor, unsure where he was going with the conversation. "That's true. So what are you planning to do?"

"I had intended to tour a local oil drilling site and hold a press conference there to present my environmental package. It is not scheduled for a few days, but I would like a preview of the place undeterred by the staff at the site." He hesitated. "And undeterred by my own."

Jane gaped at him. Darkness had fallen while he was inside, the last slivers of sunlight straining against the sky. "But it's night, Stefan. There isn't much you can tell at night."

Stefan shrugged. "Perhaps not. But I cannot sit in that suite. I am going."

Jane threw her shoulders back, bracing for a fight. "Then I'm going with you."

Stefan stared at her for a long moment, working his mouth as if fighting a protest. But in the end, his jaw went slack as if he realized arguing with her was futile.

"Very well," he said quietly. "But if there's trouble, I will handcuff you inside the car to keep you safe if necessary."

Jane's lungs tightened at his declaration.

Although an unseemly image of him handcuffing her to his bed danced through her mind, and she bit back a response. She couldn't allow him to know how he'd affected her.

It was too dangerous for her. She had to protect him from danger.

And protect herself from him.

STEFAN ALMOST SMILED at the myriad of emotions crisscrossing Jane's face. He enjoyed making the woman uncomfortable. After all, she had completely ripped him out of his own comfort zone.

"Stefan—"

"Do not respond," he said, knowing she'd have a smart retort if she did. He wanted to leave his last words in her mind to torment her.

"So, do you still wish to accompany me?" he said, his voice resonating with sexual undertones.

"I would be irresponsible if I let you go alone."

He chuckled, then pressed a finger to the tip of her nose. "And Jane Cameron is always responsible."

She started to stammer, but he brushed by her and led the way from the gardens to the front to call for a driver. But Jane closed a hand around his phone before he could make the call.

"Don't. Let me drive you."

"I told you that I do not wish to put you in harm's way."

"Stefan," Jane said. "I know you don't respect me as a criminologist—"

"I did not say that."

"You didn't have to."

He wrapped his hand around hers where she still gripped his phone. "I respect and admire you very much, Jane." He hated that his voice cracked but emotions flooded him. "That is the reason I could not stand to see you harmed."

Jane's breath gushed out, shaky and raw. "The feeling is mutual," Jane admitted. "Now listen to me. So far, you received a warning that you couldn't trust anyone. Your friend Amir has disappeared in a suspicious bombing. And you've been shot at."

Pain flickered in Stefan's eyes.

"Have you considered that the person behind this attack might be one of your own team?"

Stunned, Stefan stared at her, momentarily speechless. "My people have been checked and double-checked. All of our security teams have."

"Maybe I'm being overly cautious," Jane said.

"But give it some thought. Someone is tracking every move you've made so far, meaning an insider could be feeding them information."

How could he dismiss her suspicions when her speculations made perfect sense?

"I know it's hard to fathom," Jane continued. "But just for tonight, let me drive you. Don't tell anyone where we're going."

Tension riddled him, but he could not deny her plea. After all, they were simply going for a drive. If anyone followed, they would both be on alert.

And being alone with Jane…now, that had a special appeal all its own.

An appeal that had nothing to do with being safe or fear of an attack.

JANE SET HER GPS for directions to the oil drilling sight, her nerves on edge. Miles and miles of wilderness stretched before her, the sight of wild mustangs and antelope roaming the land reminding her of how much she loved Wyoming.

And of the problems the oil drilling had caused the environment. The air was polluted, crime had escalated, animal life was in danger.

All problems Stefan thought he could rectify.

Stefan…

She hated to make him distrustful of his own people, but the facts of the case indicated that someone might be leaking information to the royals' enemies, and she would be totally remiss in her job if she hadn't brought his attention to the matter.

He was obviously too close to his own people to see it. Which meant that she should probably get even closer so she could keep her eyes on them.

But getting closer meant insinuating herself more into his life, and that meant physically being closer to the prince.

Only being close to him was playing havoc on her nerves and seriously endangering her sanity. Because each moment she spent with him made her want him more.

Even his loyalty to his servants roused her admiration. What would she do if a man ever devoted himself to her like that?

Not the issue, Jane. Stop daydreaming.

Glancing over her shoulder, she checked to make sure no one was following them, but the traffic was thin, the road virtually deserted as she veered away from the resort. The oil-drilling site was miles from Wind River Ranch and Resort and the opposite direction of Dumont, eliminating heavy traffic. That would make it much easier to spot a tail.

Stefan sat rigid, checking the mirrors and side roads himself, honed for trouble. She saw the wheels turning in his brain and sympathized. She also recognized the tough military man who had emerged, the man who was prepared to forgo personal considerations in lieu of serving his countrymen.

Stefan would be a formidable leader. Yet he was concerned with people and the environment and he wanted peace.

Qualities that made her curious about his environmental research.

She'd been so lost in her thoughts that the scenery had passed in a blur, and she suddenly realized that it was time to make the final turn for the oil-drilling site, and she hadn't paid as much attention to the traffic as she should have.

Dammit. What if someone had followed them? She couldn't let her emotions play into the situation and endanger Stefan.

She checked the rearview mirror again and noticed headlights, but a minute later, the car swerved down a side road, and she breathed a sigh of relief. Five minutes later, she spotted the oil-drilling site ahead.

Heavy machinery, outbuildings housing equipment, supplies, and rest facilities for the workers loomed in the distance, dim lights accentuating the starkness of the area. A large hole had already been drilled for core samples and a reserve pit for wastes, eyesores and areas that could adversely affect the environment.

"You say you have answers to environmental issues," Jane said. "Environmentalists have complained that, among other issues, the oil drilling sites have altered the migration habits of the antelope."

"There is reason for concern," Stefan said quietly.

She thought of the untamed beautiful land and its wildlife population and her heart squeezed. Thousands of miles of undisturbed land devoted to animal and plant life were now being explored, upsetting the terrain and its inhabitants.

If Stefan had answers to alleviate some of these problems, the U.S. needed to listen.

She parked, climbed from the vehicle and grabbed flashlights for both of them, a soft hissing sound echoing in the air that made the hairs on her nape rise.

"What is that?" Jane asked.

"Shallow gas from the big drive pipes," Stefan explained. "Nothing to worry about, but the pressure buildup below the surface has to be monitored as the oil is drilled."

Jane nodded. She'd heard of terrible accidents, a man crushed at one Wyoming site, and knew the process was dangerous. "The workers are paid well," Jane said. "But they should be considering the risks they take."

"Risks can be minimized if proper procedures are in place," Stefan said.

"We've also had an increase in crime," Jane added, consumed with her own thoughts now. "Meth labs have become more prominent, and I've heard that many workers are using just to keep themselves awake for the long hours."

"Yes, not good," Stefan murmured as he walked through the site.

Jane shone her flashlight across the way, spotlighting trucks, pipes, chains and cables and two more mammoth holes.

"Why so many trucks?" she asked.

"One is a control truck," Stefan explained. "It controls the explosive that splits the pipes beneath the surface. Then there is a pump truck, sand truck, detergent truck, water truck…" He gestured to the individual vehicles. "All necessary and serve their own purpose."

Platforms had been built to study the oil sites, and lights erected for night drilling. Jane walked over to examine one of the outbuildings and found a rear entrance unlocked. Stefan methodically moved along the trucks and equipment as if analyzing the details, then ventured into a separate building, a metal structure she assumed held supplies.

Determined not to let Stefan out of her sight, she hurried over to the warehouse, squinting as she tried to adjust her eyes to the dark interior. The smell of machine oil, sweat and other chemicals swirled around her as she entered, a sudden wind picking up outside.

Stefan spent the next half hour studying the contents, murmuring comments of concern and points he wanted to address regarding equipment and safety procedures. In the distance, Jane thought she heard the rumble of a car, no, a motorbike. But when she checked through the doorway she saw nothing, just dust swirling in a thick fog.

Footsteps creaked across the floor, and she turned, thinking it was Stefan. But suddenly a shot blasted the air.

The bullet pinged near her, and she grabbed her weapon from her purse and pivoted, searching frantically for Stefan and the shooter but it was so dark she couldn't see. Another bullet zipped by her face, and she ducked.

"Jane!"

"Stay down," she yelled.

Spotting the shiny glint of metal from the opposite side, she crouched down and headed to Stefan, determined to get him under cover. But a thunderous roar filled the air. Then a heavy piece of metal slammed into her shoulder.

Jane screamed and struggled to remain upright, but the blow hit her jaw, she heard a tooth crack, then something slammed into her skull.

Pinpricks of lights danced in a dizzying circle in front of her before she collapsed to the ground. She fought to regain her equilibrium but lost the battle and darkness swallowed her into its abyss.

Chapter Eleven

Stefan spun around at the sound of Jane's cry, fear gnawing at his throat. Darkness shrouded the interior of the warehouse obliterating his view, but footsteps shuffled near where he'd heard Jane, so he crept toward her.

A bullet sailed by his shoulder, and he ducked to the right behind a stack of pipes. Had Jane been hit?

He crawled around the mound of pipes, searching the shadows for the shooter, then heard a low groan and spotted Jane lying in a hcap on the floor.

He had to get to her, see how badly she was injured.

Listening for the shooter, he kept low to the ground, using the stacks of pipes and cables as cover.

"Jane." He knelt beside her, panic seizing him at the sight of blood dotting her forehead.

"Dammit," Jane growled and pushed against the flooring to steady herself.

"Jane, stay still. You have a head injury."

She clutched his arm with a steely grip. "I have to go after the shooter."

He gently pushed her back down, worried about the knot swelling on her head. "You are not going anywhere right now," he hissed. "You are bleeding and probably have a concussion!"

"I'm fine," Jane protested, trying to use her feet as leverage to anchor herself to a sitting position.

He hastily removed a handkerchief from his pocket and pressed it over Jane's forehead to stem the blood flow. "If you don't stay put, I'm going to tie you down like I promised earlier," he snapped. "Now where is your gun?"

Jane must have felt dizzy because she swayed backward, and he caught her and eased her back down. "I don't know," she whispered frantically. "I lost it when I fell."

Footsteps scurried across the room again, and Stefan spotted the shooter easing toward the left side of the warehouse, slipping between rows of supplies.

He would not let this man hurt Jane any more than he already had. "Keep pressure on your head and lie still until I return."

Sweeping his hand across the flooring, he searched for Jane's gun. His hand hit a nail and tore his skin, but he ignored the pain and narrowed his eyes, searching between the rows of pipes, tubing and cables.

Finally a shiny glint flickered in the darkness, and he grabbed it then tucked it back into Jane's hands.

"Keep that ready in case he comes back."

"No, take it," Jane said.

Stefan shook his head. "I am not leaving you unarmed."

He dropped a quick kiss on her nose, then crept toward the doorway. The shooter was hiding between a supply of explosives. Panic momentarily struck him. If this guy set off those explosives, it would be all over for him and Jane.

He instantly resorted back to military mode and slowed his breathing to avoid detection. Then he padded quietly across the warehouse like a sniper tracking his mark.

He had to become one with the night. Move without sound. Blend with his surroundings. Plan and attack.

The scent of oil and other chemicals suffused the air, but he dug deeper with his senses, and smelled the musty scent of sweat and cigar.

The shooter was a smoker.

Zeroing in on his location took only a fraction of a second. He could track anyone by his scent, and this man reeked, even in light of the strong odors suffusing the warehouse.

Deciding to lead the man away from Jane, he dashed toward the back doorway nearest the shooter. The man fired, but he swerved, weaving and zigzagging until he sprinted through the door. He prayed the man would follow and Jane would be safe.

His prayers were answered when he heard footsteps racing after him. Wanting to catch the man off guard, he rushed through the exit, spun around, jumped to the side and waited. But the guy was onto him and slowed, easing around the corner with his weapon drawn.

Stefan karate-chopped his arm and the man's weapon flew from his hand, landing near the reserve pit. Stefan lunged for it, but just as his fingers closed around the handle, the shooter punched Stefan in the jaw. Stefan staggered backward slightly from the blow, but managed to hold on to the gun. But the man was fast and head butted him, then reached for the gun.

They fought and struggled, the weapon released a round into the air, then the man kneed Stefan in the groin. Stefan groaned, still clutching the gun, but the beefy jerk managed to snap his wrist with his arm and the gun sailed into the dirt somewhere a few feet away.

Anger fueled Stefan's strength, and he lunged toward the sniper. The impact sent his attacker backward, and they both flew to the ground. Dust swirled around them as they rolled and struggled, trading blow for blow. Stefan's fist connected with the man's nose and bones crunched.

"Damn you!" Blood gushed from his nose and he spit at Stefan, then threw a fist toward Stefan's stomach.

Stefan rolled again, and the man snatched his leg, trying to yank him back, but Stefan kicked at him, slamming his fist into the guy's head. A litany of curses rent the air, and Stefan reached for the gun again.

But the man got a second wind, bellowed, and jumped him from behind, slamming his body into Stefan's and dragging him into a chokehold. Somewhere in the background, he thought he heard Jane yelling his name, and an image of her bloody head flashed in his mind.

Adrenaline surged through him. He twisted, throwing punch after punch at his attacker, pried the man's beefy hands from his neck, then flipped him onto his back at the edge of the pit.

The man shouted as his body slid toward the pit. Stefan shoved him harder, and his legs went over, his hands clawing at the dirt to keep from sinking into it.

"You have to die!" the bastard yelled.

Stefan's fingers closed around the man's weapon, and he aimed it at his face.

"You won't do it," the sniper ground out, his face ruddy with rage and covered in dirt. In the fight, Stefan had ripped the man's shirt, and moonlight played across some kind of tattoo on the man's chest. A cathedral.

Stefan frowned. He'd heard that Russian tattoos held meaning, that the number of steeples on a cathedral tattoo indicated the number of years or times a man had been incarcerated.

Stefan stood, the gun still pointed at the burly man's face, and stepped on his fingers. He yelped in pain, but Stefan increased the pressure, moving the weapon so the nuzzle pressed against the man's temple.

"Who hired you to kill me?" Stefan growled.

The sniper spit at Stefan's feet, and Stefan shoved his head with the tip of the gun. "Tell me or so help me I will put a bullet through your brain."

One of the man's hands slipped, and he swung sideways. "You'll kill me anyway."

Stefan stomped harder on the man's fingers, grounding his heels in painfully. "That tattoo means you're part of the Russian mob. Who sent you here?"

Suddenly the man swung his other hand up at Stefan's ankle, and a sharp pain sliced through Stefan's leg. The bastard had pulled a knife and stabbed him.

The blow caught Stefan off guard, and his leg buckled, giving the man just enough time to throw himself from the pit. But instead of attacking Stefan, he ran back toward the warehouse where Jane was.

The bastard intended to use her as leverage.

Over his dead body.

Stefan's ankle throbbed, but he ignored the pain and aimed at the Russian. He could not let him get to Jane.

Clenching his teeth, he fired, but the bully disappeared inside the warehouse. Stefan heaved a breath, slowed as he approached the building in case the guy was waiting to ambush him again, then held the gun at the ready as he slowly inched inside.

"Jane?" He cast a quick look sideways and noticed she wasn't lying where he'd left her. A silent prayer rolled off his tongue. She had to be safe.

A loud noise sounded, pipes rolling. Then out of the darkness the sniper jumped toward him, swinging a heavy pipe. Stefan fired again, and the man bellowed as the bullet connected with his chest. The Russian lunged sideways with another curse, but slammed into a wall of pipes.

"Stefan, get out of the way!" Jane yelled.

Then he heard it—the rumbling as the pipes began to crash down on top of the sniper. The man collapsed, throwing up his arms to protect himself against the onslaught, but the mounds of metal and steel pelted him, pinning him to the floor and crushing him.

"Jane?" Stefan spun around searching for her.

Jane flew from behind the massive metal pile and launched herself into his arms. Stefan wrapped his arms around her and held on to her.

JANE CLUNG TO STEFAN, afraid if she released him he might disappear again. And that this time he might not come back.

"I thought that he had you," Stefan whispered, pulling her closer to him and nuzzling her hair. "That he might have hurt you."

She shook her head, her breath uneven as she fought back a sob. "And I was afraid he'd shot you. Or worse..." She couldn't even speak the words out loud.

Stefan dying was not an option.

"No, I am unharmed." He tilted her head backward and kissed the swollen bruise on her forehead. "When I think you could have been killed, it makes me insane."

Tears blurred her eyes. Dammit, she never cried. But her head was pounding as if someone had taken a sledgehammer to it. Come to think of it, that might have been what the bastard used.

"You need a doctor," Stefan said, then gently stroked the matted hair away from her face. "And this time you will allow them to examine you."

Jane glanced down at Stefan's torn pants and the blood dotting the floor beside his shoe. "My God, Stefan. You're the one who needs medical treatment."

She pulled away, then stooped to examine his wound. Stefan dropped to his knees and gripped her by the arms. "Jane, stop—"

"No, let me see how deep the cut is." She quickly shoved up his pants, then gasped at the bloody gash. "You need stitches."

"I'll live. We need to figure out how this guy found us."

Jane punched in the sheriff's number. "Sheriff Wolf, this is Jane Cameron." She explained about the dead man and requested an ambulance.

"I'm on my way and so is an ambulance," the sheriff said. "Do you need another CSI team?"

"Yes," Jane said. "If we can match the bullet casings and the man's prints, we'll know he's the same sniper who shot at us earlier and killed Stefan's guard."

"But someone set him up to it," Stefan said as she disconnected the call. "This man served time in prison. He is a hired killer."

"Just as we suspected from the sniper weapon." Jane nodded. "Now we tend to your injury."

Stefan pushed away her hands. "I refuse to be treated like an invalid when you are suffering a head injury," Stefan said curtly. "Now, I will sit only if you join me."

Jane sighed, part disgusted with the way he wanted to boss her around. Part dizzy from the blow to her temple and aching to have Stefan's arms around her again.

"All right," she conceded.

Laughter rumbled from him as he wrapped his arm around her.

"What's so funny?" Jane asked as they hobbled outside and parked themselves on a cluster of rocks.

He squeezed her to him, then cupped her face between his hands. "It is difficult for you to accept someone actually taking care of you, is it not?"

She stared up into his eyes, blinking back moisture and hating the vulnerability this case—and Stefan—brought out in her.

"Yes."

"Because you have always had to stand on your own?"

She chewed her bottom lip. "There's nothing wrong with that."

He stroked her hair as he pulled her into his embrace. "Oh, Jane, I am going to make your life so difficult."

"What do you mean?" Jane whispered.

He pulled her so close his breath bathed her cheek. Then he laid his head against hers, holding her close, so close she heard his heart beating in his chest, and felt the fine tremor of nerves in his fingers as they brushed her cheek. "I am going to take care of you tonight."

Jane's first instinct was to push him away, to run. "Stefan, no—"

"Shh." He pressed his lips gently to hers, a teasing sensation that stirred baser needs.

There were no cameras here now. No one to see that she was leaning on this man. No one to laugh that plain Jane was in the arms of a prince.

There was only the peaceful night air, the sounds of wild animals roaming across the land, of birds of prey and night owls and insects buzzing with life and the sound of his breath assuring her she was alive.

Stefan was strong, a man with a mission, a man who wanted to help his country but also share his environmental research to preserve this land that she loved.

So she curled into his arms and let him hold her until the ambulance arrived.

STEFAN SAVORED the feel of Jane in his arms, and simply held her for what seemed like endless time. But more than the titillating sensation of her cheek against his chest, he treasured the fact that this brave woman had just given him her trust.

He sensed her trust was a rare commodity, a gift to treasure. And it meant far more to him than any woman's solicitous advances or taking Jane to bed.

Although he certainly desired to do that.

A siren wailed in the distance, the twirling

lights of emergency vehicles and the sheriff's SUV brightening the dark sky. Jane sighed in his arms, both of them having grown comfortable and relaxed.

He hated the intrusion.

Yet even as he held her, his mind was haunted by the attack on Amir. By the murder of his security agent Benito. By the attack here tonight.

And as the sheriff arrived, the medics tended to his ankle and Jane, then the CSI agents began to process the scene and gather forensics, questions plagued him along with details that he couldn't deny. Jane's comment about an insider leaking information niggled at his brain.

Who had known where he was going?

Jane glanced at him from where she sat with a bandage on her head on the gurney, and a sickening feeling clawed at his gut.

Other than Jane, there were only two people who had been privy of his plans for the evening.

Two people he trusted with his life.

And one of them might have given the orders to have him killed.

Chapter Twelve

"We need to transport the prince to the hospital for stitches," one of the paramedics told Jane.

Jane turned to Osgood, who had arrived shortly after the sheriff and coroner. "I should accompany him until his security team can meet us there."

"Fine," Osgood said. "Tomas and I will handle the crime scene here." Tomas was photographing and tagging the sites where he located bullet fragments and casings. He'd discovered a motorbike in the woods which had obviously been the sniper's way in.

Jane joined Stefan where he sat on a stretcher. He looked angry and obstinate.

"I do not wish to go to the hospital," he said stiffly. "I need to speak with my security team at once."

"After your ankle is treated." Jane laid a hand on his shoulder, hoping to assuage his frustration. "The last thing you want is to get an infection from this stab wound and end up on bed rest, unable to attend the summit when things settle down."

He pressed his lips together but conceded, obviously seeing the logic of her point.

Still, as the medics hoisted him into the ambulance, he grumbled, "I've had worse injuries than this and walked away without treatment."

Jane climbed in beside him, stowing her weapon in her shoulder bag. But as the medics raced toward the hospital, she kept her eyes trained out the back to make certain no one was on their tail.

"Do you want me to call your security and explain what happened?" Jane asked.

Stefan shook his head. "No. I will hold a meeting when I return to the resort. I want to see each of their faces when I relay this incident."

"Then you do suspect someone on your team of leaking your location?"

Stefan ran a hand through his thick dark hair. "I do not wish to, but I must."

Compassion for him filled Jane. Confronting his co-workers, friends and staff would be difficult for Stefan. She hoped that one of his men—or his friends—hadn't betrayed him.

But if they discovered the person who'd

ordered the attacks was amongst them, she wouldn't hesitate to make an arrest.

TENSION THRUMMED through Stefan as the doctor cleaned and stitched his ankle. He mentally reviewed the details of the last few weeks in his head, and could not believe where his train of thought was taking him.

When they first arrived, Jane had explained to the doctor about the shooting, swearing him to secrecy.

"Don't worry," the doctor said. "We adhere to a strict patient-confidentiality rule here. You don't have to worry about anyone on my staff communicating with the press."

"Thank you," Stefan said, although he had a bad feeling the media would find out anyway. Somehow the American press and paparazzi had the senses of a vulture, and the electronic means to invade their privacy at the most inopportune moments.

Just as the doctor finished bandaging his ankle, a nurse appeared with a wheelchair.

"I am perfectly capable of walking," Stefan said, ignoring the pain as he stood and forced himself to put weight on his ankle in order to prove his point. He was a soldier, not a helpless invalid.

He could not afford weakness.

"Don't argue," Jane said with a small smile. "It's hospital policy." She patted her purse where she had stowed her weapon. "Besides, we've mapped out a route to sneak you out of here without the press seeing."

"The media is outside?"

Jane nodded. "Afraid so. Danny Harold is waiting at the front door, camera ready." She pointed to the chair. "So just sit down, Stefan. And let me get you back to the resort."

Stefan growled but dropped into the chair, anxious to leave. Jane led the way, checking the corridors and ducking around corners until they exited through a back delivery door. Her SUV was waiting.

"How did you retrieve your vehicle?" Stefan asked.

"The sheriff had one of his men drop it off. Get in."

He bit back a retort as she helped him stand, then he slid into the passenger seat. A minute later, Jane fastened her seat belt and drove toward the exit. He checked the sides and rear entrance, expecting to see the media, but Jane's plan seemed to work.

Behind him, he spotted the whirling lights of

another ambulance arriving, and the rush of the media swarming toward it.

He would have chuckled at her cunning plan had he not been tied in knots over the fact that one of his people might have deceived him. "Very good job, Jane," he murmured.

She glanced at him, a frown marring her forehead. "How are you feeling?"

He zeroed in on the bruise on her cheek and bandage on her forehead. "Like I'm going to tear someone apart if I find out they deceived me and masterminded these attacks."

Jane clamped her teeth over her bottom lip, but didn't reply. Instead she focused on the highway, giving him time to assimilate his thoughts as they drove to the resort.

The sky was dark, the moon almost nonexistent, making the twinkling lights of the resort dance in the sky as they approached. Stefan texted Edilio and asked him to meet him in the office of his suite and requested Hector be present as well.

Jane parked in the private parking spot beside his cottage, visually scanning the area as she went in. Stefan did the same. Jane thought she was protecting him, but he'd already decided that keeping her close to him was the only way he could be assured of her safety.

The last thing he wanted was for someone to use her as a bargaining chip to get to him.

Seconds later, he stood in the office of his suite, staring at Edilio and Hector.

Edilio's stern dark brows pinched together. "Prince Stefan, what happened?"

"Miss Cameron and I were ambushed tonight at the oil drilling site." Stefan glanced back and forth between his head of security and his chief aide and loyal friend. "And you two were the only ones who knew of my plans tonight."

Hector paled and pressed a hand to his chest, gulping for a breath. Edilio squared his shoulders, his body rigid, his face a mask of steel.

"What are you suggesting, Prince?" Edilio asked. "That one of us betrayed you?"

Stefan's chest ached more severely than his ankle. "I have to ask. We weren't followed, so that indicates that someone on my staff might have leaked my whereabouts to this sniper."

Edilio clicked his heels. "I would never betray you, Prince. I am as always your loyal employee." He removed his weapon and extended it to Stefan. "But if you wish to have me removed from your presence and incarcerated to prove that point, then I relinquish my weapon to you."

Hector's expression looked tormented. "Prince…"

"Hector?" Stefan's body went numb with shock as fear set in. "Hector, are you all right?"

Hector sank into a chair, rubbing his chest and wheezing for a breath. "I'm sorry, sir, I'm sorry…" His voice trailed off as emotions overcame him.

Jane felt his pulse. "It's weak and thready. Did you leak the prince's whereabouts, Hector?"

Hector groaned, his head lolling back slightly, his complexion a pasty white.

"Hector?" Stefan asked. "Tell me this minute what you have done."

Tears blurred the old man's eyes, and Edilio moved to his side as well, his stance aggressive as if he planned to attack if Hector tried to bolt.

But Hector gasped for air, rocking forward in the chair. Jane caught him and helped him sit back, then glanced at Stefan, panic in her eyes. "I think he's having a heart attack," Jane said quietly. "I'll call a doctor."

She stepped aside to use the phone, and Stefan knelt by the old man. "Hector, tell me what's going on. You have been my father's friend, my friend, why would you do this?"

"They have…my family." Hector made a

choking sound. "They...threatened to k...ill them."

Stefan's blood ran cold. "What do you mean? Who has your family?"

Hector closed his eyes and swayed, and terror streaked through Stefan. "Hector, tell me who has them."

"Don't know," Hector rasped. "Called me, told me I had to help them or else..." He choked on a breath.

Jane rushed over and loosened Hector's collar. "Dr. Leonard, the doctor on call for the resort, will be right here."

Stefan wiped perspiration from Hector's brow, remembering Hector doing the same for his father when he'd first become ill. Hector watching over him when he was a child. Hector and his family sharing holidays with his family. Hector bouncing his baby granddaughter on his knee. "Do you know who has them, Hector, or where they are holding them?"

Hector shook his head. "No... So sorry, Prince Stefan...couldn't let them die..." Fear, sorrow, regret thickened his voice. "Didn't mean for Benito to get killed. God forgive me..."

Hector started to cry then, a big wailing sob that ripped at Stefan's gut.

A knock sounded at the door, and Jane rushed

to open it. "Dr. Leonard." Jane gestured for him to enter. "Mr. Perro is over here. I think he's having a heart attack."

Stefan patted Hector's shoulder. "Do not worry, my friend. I will find your family and make sure they are safe." He stood so the doctor could examine Hector then turned to Edilio.

"Have one of our men guard him at all times. And monitor any calls he receives."

Edilio nodded and Stefan knotted his hands into fists. If Hector or his family died, he would make certain whoever was responsible suffered for their crimes.

JANE'S MIND RACED. She hated the pain on Stefan's face, but Hector obviously cared a great deal for him and betraying him had cost him big time.

It might even cost him his family, too.

She had to do something to help.

"Let me see Hector's cell phone," she said.

Stefan frowned, distressed, and Jane's heart ached for him. If Hector's family was hurt or murdered because of him, Stefan would suffer as well.

"Stefan, the phone," Jane said. "Maybe we can trace whoever threatened Hector."

Her words seem to jar him out of his shock, and he nodded. "Of course."

Edilio reached inside the man's pocket and retrieved the cell phone. Dr. Leonard gave Hector an aspirin and was checking his vitals as the ambulance arrived and two medics rushed inside.

Jane punched the number for the crime lab and requested a trace be placed on Hector's number in case he received any more calls. Then she began to search the phone log as the medics loaded a despondent Hector onto the gurney and rushed him to the ambulance.

"You can go with him if you like," Jane said, humbled by the concern on Stefan's face. Even though Hector was an employee, Stefan obviously cared for him as family.

"No," Edilio spoke up. "I will go. If he knows any more than he's said, I will call."

"One more thing," Stefan said. "Have you heard anything about Jarryd or Butrus?"

Edilio lowered his voice. "According to sources, Jarryd is rallying against the summit but there's nothing specific indicating he's involved in the attacks. Not so far anyway. And Butrus—according to an inside man, he is in favor of the summit. As far as opposing the marriage, he has kept his reasons to himself."

"Interesting. Keep me posted."

As Edilio left, Stefan turned to Jane. "What can you tell from the phone, Jane?"

She scrolled through the history of calls. "There are a few calls to you. And this number." She angled the display screen for Stefan to read the number.

"Edilio's personal cell."

"How about this one?" Jane asked, gesturing to an *unknown* number.

"I do not recognize it," Stefan said.

Jane tried calling it back. "Damn," she muttered. "It's blocked. Could be from a prepaid throwaway cell or someone smart enough to know how to keep us from tracing them."

"Can you do something?"

She nodded. "I'll send it to Computer Crimes at the lab. One of our experts might be able to trace it."

Stefan paced the room. "So what do we do now?" He threw his hands up, agitated. "What if this attack was about me all along? What if the bomb that struck the limo with Amir was intended for me? This bastard does not care who he hurts as long as destroys me."

He gripped her arms. "Please, Jane. Excuse yourself from the investigation."

Jane brushed his cheek with the palm of her

hand. "Stefan, you're panicking, letting fear control you. We can't do that or they win."

Stefan hissed, then strode to the window and looked out, his shoulders tense, his head bowed in thought.

Jane cleared her throat. "While I go arrange a courier to get this phone to the lab, think about the people you know, the enemies you listed, about who would know to target Hector's family."

She quickly punched in the number for the courier service and requested a transfer of evidence, then disconnected and exited the room to meet the courier.

Hopefully Stefan would come up with a lead while she was gone. If not, maybe Computer Crimes could find a link to the kidnapper.

That might be the break they needed to bust this case wide open and find the sheik.

Hector's agonized face haunted Stefan. He had to find his family. They were in danger because of him.

He punched in the number for his father's security team in Kyros. Julius Kassar, his father's personal security agent, answered.

"It is Stefan. I need to verify that my father

and brother are safe," Stefan said, tensing as he waited.

"Your father is resting well. Your brother just left with his own guard. What about you, Prince? We heard news of a bombing, and that you were fired upon."

"Yes, but I am okay." Stefan rolled his shoulders, then explained about Hector. "I need your men to determine if the Perro family has been taken hostage," Stefan said. "If they have, I need you to locate them and devise a rescue plan."

Julius made a clicking sound with his teeth. "Yes, sir. I will assign men to it immediately. Do you have any idea where the kidnapper might be holding the family?"

"No. Check the house first. Then...use your resources." He contemplated the possibilities. "The American police are analyzing Hector's phone to trace the source. If they are successful, maybe it will lead us to that location." Stefan rubbed a hand over the back of his neck. "And, Julius, please call me as soon as you know anything."

A knock sounded at the door, and Stefan snapped his phone closed. "Yes?"

"It's me, Jane."

"Come in."

She opened the door, the bruise on her face

stark against her pale skin. This woman was tough and strong, but she had been through hell and back, had worked around the clock because of him, and continued to amaze him with her skills and fortitude.

"You sent the phone to the lab?" he asked.

Jane nodded. "Hopefully they can find out who made that call and where it came from."

He closed the distance between them, suddenly needing to be near her. "I phoned my security team in Kyros. They are searching for Hector's family."

"Good. I hope they're unharmed," Jane said. "I know you're upset about what Hector did, but under the circumstances..."

"Yes, under the circumstances..." Anguish rocked through Stefan at the mere thought of Hector's family suffering. At the thought of Hector dying because he'd been coerced into helping Stefan's enemy.

But it was obvious that whoever orchestrated the attacks would hurt anyone to kill him.

Including Jane.

This time he would not accept no for an answer. He had to get her removed from this investigation, even if he had to tie her down and endure her wrath to do so.

Chapter Thirteen

"You have done your duty, now leave," Stefan said curtly. "I do not wish you to continue working this case. If need be, I will phone the sheriff or whomever necessary to have you replaced."

Jane gaped at him. She knew he was upset about Hector and his family, but was he blaming her? "What are you blabbering about? You think this is my fault?"

"I have my own people to protect me. Having you here is a distraction." Stefan jerked his head back, annoyed. "I demand you remove yourself from this investigation, and this time I will not accept your protests."

His icy tone took Jane by surprise, but anguish tinged his tone. Stefan blamed himself for endangering his friend and his family, for Benito's death. And he was trying to protect her.

In his own alpha male kind of way.

It was a chivalrous gesture, but her temper flared.

"Stefan, you aren't in Kyros. You can't order me around."

"But—"

She pressed a finger to his lips to quiet him. "I am a grown woman, a trained professional. I intend to do my job, and nothing you do or say will deter me."

A muscle ticked in his jaw. "I could tie you down. Lock you in my quarters until this situation is resolved."

His concern not only touched her, but the gruff texture of his voice and his threat to tie her down triggered wicked fantasies that she'd never imagined before. Fantasies that heated her blood and made her crave his touch.

"I understand you feel responsible," Jane said softly. "That you're torn up about your friends being hurt and endangered. But I can take care of myself, Stefan."

A charged moment passed between them. Jane wanted Stefan to accept her for herself. There was no other way they could be together…

Not that they had a future.

God, what was wrong with her? Suddenly seeing images of her and Stefan in love, marrying, having a family.

That scenario would never happen.

But she could comfort him tonight. Have a night in his arms.

"Jane...you have already suffered two injuries," Stefan said on a hushed breath. "Do you not understand? I could not tolerate it if you were hurt further."

His voice cracked, and Jane's heart melted. She had never had a man worry about her.

"Stefan..." Jane pressed her hand to his cheek. "Thank you for your concern, for being the man you are. But I'm tough, and I want to be here, to help."

Stefan's breath gushed out. "Don't you see, Jane? If you left, I would not have to worry about you anymore."

Jane traced her finger along his jaw. "I'm not leaving you, Stefan. I'm here for you now."

His face twisted in turmoil. "But I need you safe."

"I'm safe with you," Jane murmured.

Stefan stared at her for a long moment, the stark emotions in his eyes making her want to soothe him.

She lifted one of his hands and kissed it, hoping to show him that she could be tender as well as strong.

Then suddenly Stefan's wall seem to crumble,

he yanked Jane into his arms and crushed her in his embrace. "I wish to keep you that way," he murmured next to her ear. "In one beautiful unharmed piece, here with me."

Jane closed her eyes, imagining that he was speaking of forever when she knew plain girls like her didn't get forever.

When the danger was over and Stefan closed his business deals, he'd go home to Kyros and marry some exotic princess.

But tonight he was hers.

STEFAN'S RESISTANCE FLED. He had desired Jane from the first moment he'd seen her. Knowing that she wanted him now only fueled his passion to a burning crescendo. He had almost lost her earlier.

He had to have her now.

A sultry smile curled her lips, and he angled his head and claimed her mouth with his. She tasted like sweetness and stubborn vulnerability, and raw sexuality. He traced his tongue along the seam of her lips, probing, teasing, aching until she parted her lips wider and suckled his tongue into her mouth. Together their tongues danced, a symphony of erotic moves that made his body rock hard and begging to be inside hers.

Jane ran her hands along his shoulder blades,

stroking his back and rubbing her femininity against the v of his thighs, and his erection thickened, pressing against his slacks to the point of pain.

He trailed his lips across her throat, nibbling at the tender skin behind her ear. She moaned softly, and stroked his calf with her foot. Passion exploded inside him, and he traced his tongue along her neck.

"Jane?" he whispered.

"Yes."

He brushed hair away from her neck. "I want to make love to you," Stefan murmured.

"Oh, yes," she whispered. "Please."

Stefan smiled at the husky sound of her admission then swept her up into his arms and carried her to his bed. He threw the coverlet aside and eased her onto the white satin sheets, drawing back slightly to look into her face.

Her eyes flared with passion, the rosy hue to her cheeks a sign of her arousal. "You are exquisite," he said softly.

Jane started to shake her head, but he bent and kissed her, cutting off any response. He refused to hear her berate herself.

He was a man and he knew better than she.

She purred into his mouth, rubbing against him in invitation, and he lowered one hand to peel away her clothes. The material slipped off her shoulders, and she wrestled out of it. He tossed it onto the ottoman beside the bed, then let his eyes rove over her voluptuous body.

Her breasts spilled over the scalloped edges of her black lacy bra, her nipples jutting against the thin barrier. He licked his lips, his chest clenching as excitement seared his blood.

Jane's eyes flared with a wantonness he had never seen before, and she began loosening the buttons on his shirt.

"I want to touch you," Jane whispered hoarsely.

Pleasure rippled through him at her husky admission. Nothing had ever sounded so sweet to his ears as her declaration.

"And I want to love every inch of you, my darling."

A blush crept onto her cheeks, and he lowered his mouth and kissed her again, another improper princely kiss that hinted at the pleasures to come.

She ripped off his shirt, and ran her hands over his chest, igniting fiery sensations along his skin with her touch. He traced his mouth over her throat and neck, then lower to tease at her cleavage, then slipped the edge of her bra back to expose one creamy breast.

She groaned and undulated her hips beneath him, and a frenzy of emotions overcame him. This woman was so much more than she seemed. So much more than any woman he had ever known.

He stripped away her bra, then her jeans. The rasp of his zipper as she undressed him flooded him with erotic sensations.

Need and longing vibrated between them as they tossed clothes and underclothes across the floor and their naked bodies slid together. He nibbled at her breasts, then suckled one plump rosy nipple into his mouth. She thrust her hips upward, then wrapped her legs around him as he laved one breast then the other.

His body hummed with arousal as his thick length wedged itself between her thighs, begging to be inside her.

But he forced himself to wait. He intended to pleasure Jane thoroughly tonight, to hear her cry in ecstasy. It would be music to his ears.

So he dipped his head lower, spreading tongue lashes down her abdomen, tasting the alluring softness of her skin as he spread her legs apart.

Jane pulled at him to join her, but he was in charge, and he refused to rush. Too many things were rushed in America. Morning coffee, dinner, sex.

Lovemaking should be long and languid and savored just as fine wine and a gourmet meal.

Her heady scent enveloped him, and he licked her belly, teasing her inner thighs with his fingers first, then gently caressing her femininity with his tongue.

Jane moaned and rolled her hips, inviting more, and he teased and stroked her, wetting her thighs with his mouth and circling her precious nub until she threaded her fingers in his hair and cried out in sweet release.

Stefan drank in her luscious flavor, his body aching for more as he finally rose above her.

"Stefan…" Jane whispered.

There was no need for words. Their bodies spoke their own silent language.

A tenderness for her surged through him, and he knew that tonight was special for both of them, that Jane did not give herself lightly or without emotion.

Pausing above her, he reached inside the nightstand, removed a condom and tore off the wrapper with his teeth. Jane watched him, her eyes awash with arousal.

He wanted her more than he had ever wanted

a woman. He wanted to be inside her, wanted to love her, wanted to make her his.

Wanted to keep her by his side forever.

The thought sent a streak of fear bolting through him. But Jane wrapped her fingers around his sex, then took the condom and slowly rolled it over his length, and fear fled.

The almost desperate hunger in her eyes as she watched him pulse in her hands nearly made him burst. He sucked air between his teeth to regain control, then pushed her hand away, cupped her bottom with his hands and yanked her hips upward.

Moaning with unspent desire, he stroked her sweetness with his throbbing length, watching elation darken her eyes as her second climax built. She moved against him, rubbing his chest, clawing at his arms, and undulating below him until he felt the first tremors of another climax gripping her body.

The desire to mate with her surged through him, and he thrust inside her. The first touch of his body inside hers felt like a fire had been lit. His body burst to life, singing with erotic sensations while his heart swelled in his chest.

Inside Jane, he had found where he belonged.

And he never wanted to leave.

Jane rasped his name, and he slid out, then

thrust again, repeating the motion as his own climax gained momentum. He stroked her over and over, pushing deeper, filling her and pulling out only to fill her again even deeper. She wrapped her legs around him, and he rocked inside her, a gruff shout of her name escaping his lips as her muscles clenched around his, and she began to climax yet again.

Adrenaline mixed with emotions as he pumped harder and faster, harder and faster, deeper and deeper until he knew she was his and he hers.

Then and only then did he allow himself to spill his seed inside her.

Yet in the afterglow of their lovemaking, fear clawed at his chest. He felt as if he'd just lost a part of himself to Jane, a part of his heart.

But a lifetime, a marriage to Jane would never work. She was a forensics specialist, an American who would never fit into his country and his world.

And if duty necessitated, he would have to do the honorable thing and follow his father's wishes and marry Daria...

His throat clogged at the thought.

JANE CURLED into Stefan's arms, sated and happier than she had ever been in her life. Stefan made her feel beautiful both inside and out, cherished and cared for and totally feminine.

But she knew it wouldn't last. Standing next to the prince, she'd be the drab wallpaper she'd always been when her glamorous mother made appearances before her death. She did not want to be in the limelight. To have people across the world gossiping and wondering why Prince Stefan had a plain girl like her on his arm. He deserved someone more worthy of being his princess.

Hush, Jane. Just enjoy the moment.

Stefan stroked her bare shoulder, drawing sensations that made her snuggle closer to him and nibble at his jaw. He angled his face to look at her, and the raw need in his eyes robbed her breath.

With moonlight spilling across his face, he looked like a fierce Greek warrior, a leader who could command an army—and a woman—with just one word. One look.

One touch.

He caressed her cheek, his breath bathing her face, and with that touch she was his, totally succumbing to his every command, to his every need.

She could lose herself so quickly in him.

Then she would be crushed when he left.

And he *would* leave.

But he kissed her again, and she finally understood her mother's obsession for love and romance, because she didn't care.

Hunger washed over her as he trailed more kisses along her jaw then flipped her over to trail them down her back and lower. And when he rolled her to her hands and knees and probed her hips apart with his thick length, she spread herself and welcomed him inside her again, crying out his name as he pumped inside her and brought her to another mind-blowing orgasm.

He growled his own pleasure, gripping her hips and burying himself so deeply that pain and pleasure mingled together, until she knew that no other man could ever fill her the way that Stefan had.

And when they were both spent, he collapsed against her, then cradled her in his arms and wrapped his legs around her. They lay there entwined, their breathing rasping in the still night air, moonlight streaming through the window as the wild animals outside roamed freely, and the honeysuckle scented the air.

It was the most beautiful night Jane had ever known. If only it would last…

But fairy tales were for dreamers. And Jane Cameron was not a fairy-tale kind of girl.

LONG INTO THE NIGHT Stefan watched Jane sleep, troubled by the emotions churning through him. He wanted Jane in his life, to love her the way she deserved to be loved. To carry her back to Kyros and share the beauty of his country with her.

To show the world what a treasure he had found in this woman. Jane was like the rarest pearl plucked from deep within an oyster shell at the bottom of the ocean.

And she was his.

Whether she understood that yet or not.

Her cell phone buzzed, and Jane jerked awake, her eyes startled. "Stefan?"

"It is your phone, Jane. Do you wish to answer?"

She shoved a strand of hair from her face and sat up, her breasts swaying and making him hard all over again. Her body was perfect, angelic, golden with curves that sent need surging through him.

"Yes, it could be about the case."

He should have turned off the phone, kept them cocooned here together where she was safe, kept her in his bed and in his arms where nothing could harm her.

But Amir and Hector's family were missing, so he resigned himself and handed her the phone.

Jane quickly connected the call. "Jane Cameron speaking." She wrinkled her nose in a frown. "I'll be right there."

She stood and grabbed her clothes.

At her anxious look, Stefan did the same. "What is going on?"

"Tomas has something he wants me to look at regarding the bomb particles."

Stefan dragged on his shirt. "Then we shall go."

Jane hesitated. "Stefan, stay here with your guard while I check it out."

Stefan's jaw tightened. "No. You are not going anywhere without me."

Jane opened her mouth to argue, but Stefan pressed a kiss to her mouth. "Do not bother to protest. I need to see this evidence your CSI speaks of."

Jane reluctantly nodded, grabbed her purse and they headed outside just as dawn started to break. Stefan texted Edilio to alert him where he was going and that Jane was with him, then she drove them to the lab.

Tomas met Jane with a perplexed look on his face. "Come here just a minute, Jane."

"I'll be right back, Stefan."

Stefan hated being left out of the loop, but that Osgood imbecile had pointed out that he was not authorized to be in the lab. Still, Jane would share what she knew with him, and show him this evidence. He would insist.

She stepped from the room, and he paced to the window and glanced outside. Morning sunlight poured across the asphalt as the city of Dumont awakened. Traffic was thickening, pedestrians bustling down the sidewalk with their disposable cups of coffee.

No time to relax or enjoy a quiet meal as in Kyros where pleasure and relaxation were priorities each day.

Still it was a beautiful day here, a day when he and his friends should have been conducting business instead of hiding out and wondering if Amir was dead or alive.

The door squeaked open, and another CSI tech, a young female who looked to be just out of university, stepped inside. When she spotted him, she blushed and graced him with a flirtatious smile. "Prince Stefan…I wasn't expecting to see you here."

He shrugged. "Yes, well, Miss Cameron and I are working together."

"Really?" The young girl's eyes went up in surprise.

"Yes. Unfortunately there has been trouble since my friends and I arrived."

"I know, and I'm so sorry." She fidgeted with the file in her hand yet her gaze roved over him in open admiration as if she wanted to touch him. "I don't understand why some people are so prejudiced. I, for one, am thrilled to have so many royals and sheiks here in the U.S."

He chuckled. She was another gushing young girl, the type he was sure that he could charm and have if he wanted.

But Jane's face flashed in his mind, and he dismissed the idea of ever wanting another woman.

"Do you have something you wish to discuss with Jane?" he asked, suddenly anxious for her to leave.

She pushed the file forward, then placed it on Jane's desk. "Yes. The information she wanted about the cell phone is in there."

Adrenaline surged through Stefan. "I shall tell her that you left it."

"Oh, I'm not in a hurry," she said. "I can wait."

Stefan took her arm and guided her to the door. A flicker of sexual interest charged her eyes, but the sultry, unspoken promise did not arouse him at all.

After all, she was not Jane.

And he certainly could not go from making love to Jane to crawling into bed with another woman.

"That is not necessary," Stefan said. "But thank you, miss. Now I would not want to get you in trouble by keeping you from your work. And as much as I am enjoying your lovely company, I have business to attend to myself."

Her eyes narrowed into a frown as if she didn't quite understand what was going on, that he was subtly rejecting her. But he gently ushered her through the door and closed it behind her.

Intent on finding out what was in that file, he hurried back and opened it. A detailed list of phone numbers from Hector's phone was inside.

He scanned the numbers. Then suddenly a jolt of fear shot through him.

One number had been circled as if in question. A number that had phoned Hector repeatedly. A number from within the States.

From within this very CSI office.

Chapter Fourteen

Osgood. His name was there, plain and clear.

The CSI who worked with Jane had phoned Hector. But why? If Osgood wanted to speak with his security detail, he would have phoned Edilio.

Stefan balled his hands into fists, rage tightening every muscle in his body. The man had some explaining to do. Stefan could think of no reason for them to have had contact unless Osgood was behind the threats on Hector's family.

Trust no one.

The warning had proven to be true. His own aide had been coerced into deceiving him. What if Osgood was corrupt?

He had to find him and make the man explain.

And he wanted to do it without Jane.

Leaving the file on the desk, he scribbled a note to Jane that he went to make a call, then strode down the hall in search of Osgood's office.

JANE FROWNED as she studied the tests Tomas had run. He was a computer whiz and research fanatic, and had studied the list of all the particles they had discovered and insisted he'd found something interesting.

"This type of material is being tested in some foreign countries," he said. "Of course, that research is under the table."

This she already knew from Stefan. "Because it has to do with nuclear weapons."

He frowned as if he hadn't expected her to know. "Yes. Biochemical warfare to be exact." Tomas pointed to several notations on the diagrams of molecules and test studies. "They've had trouble using this one though," Tomas said. "Because of the side effects exposure causes to those who work with it."

"What side effects?" Jane asked.

"Skin rashes, bleeding from the nose, eye problems, even facial muscle spasms."

Jane rubbed her forehead in thought. "Skin rashes?"

"Yes. Rashes can appear anywhere on the body, but are especially prevalent on areas of contact such as the hands and arms."

Jane's mind began to race.

"And those are the more visible problems. Long term exposure causes cancer, urinary problems, seizures, heart arrhythmia and eventually death."

Disturbing snippets of past moments with Osgood jolted through Jane's mind. Osgood scratching at his arms. His long sleeved-shirt riding up to reveal red splotches.

He'd claimed it was eczema.

And one day a few weeks back he'd had a nosebleed. He'd commented that he'd had them since childhood whenever he got a sinus infection. She had dismissed the incident and accepted his reasoning.

But now she wondered...

No, surely Osgood wouldn't betray his country.... And he wouldn't indulge in terrorism or a murder plot.

But her comment to Stefan about not suspecting the people he was close to echoed in her ears. She'd never considered suspecting anyone in her own office.

Her mind spinning, she thanked Tomas, grabbed a copy of the printouts to show Stefan and hurried from the room. The lab seemed eerily quiet, but downstairs she heard footsteps as other workers arrived at the courthouse.

She veered into her lab eager to talk to Stefan, but he was gone.

A quick scan of the room and she discovered

his note. Dammit, he'd left without a guard. Then she noticed the file on her desk, picked it up and opened the folder.

The numbers from Hector's phone.

She quickly skimmed the list, noting the out-of-area numbers which according to the computer lab, were Hector's home number. He must have been desperate, frantic when he thought his family was in danger, and had tried to call them dozens of times in the last two days. But each call indicated that the connection had lasted less than a minute. Just long enough for a message machine to kick on.

Then her gaze zeroed in on the number that had been circled.

Dammit. She recognized it immediately.

Her boss's private phone.

Her stomach rolled as she glanced at the note again. Stefan had been here when this file had been delivered.

What if he had seen it?

Then he hadn't gone to make a call. He'd gone to find Osgood.

She had to hurry….

She checked her watch. She knew exactly where Osgood would be. This time of morning he always stopped at the coffee shop downstairs. Osgood couldn't survive without his superstrength caffeine surge in the morning. He'd once commented that he needed it in an IV.

She punched the elevator button, but it took too long, so she dashed down the staircase to the bottom floor, rushed through the door to the corridor, then jogged down the hall to the coffee shop in the corner. The place was surprisingly empty, only the teenager working the coffee bar was inside.

Just as she spun toward the entrance, Osgood loped out, coffee in hand.

Her hand automatically fell over her purse where she kept her gun. His beefy face registered surprise, his eye beginning to spasm. A telltale sign.

One she should have paid more attention to.

"Jane, what are you doing here?" he asked.

"I need to talk to you, Ralph." She'd lost her breath on the jog down and had to pause to prepare her story before she tipped herself off. "There's evidence I need you to review."

He scoffed. "You, the elusive, independent, brilliant Jane Cameron, need *my* help?" Suspicion flared in his eyes. "Just what evidence are you talking about?"

Jane swallowed, trying to hedge, but knowing she had to confront him. "The lab found details about the bomb particles that hint at terrorist activity."

"Really?"

Jane nodded. "And the computer lab came back with phone records that support Prince Stefan's aide's story about being coerced into helping the person who attacked the prince and the sheik."

Osgood's beady eyes flitted sideways in a nervous gesture. "What exactly did these records reveal? Do we have a suspect to arrest?"

Jane met his gaze, her heart drumming like a freight train spinning off the tracks. She wanted to say yes, to slap the cuffs on him, but her training and self-preservation instincts kicked it. It would be better, smarter, to do it upstairs where she had backup.

"I don't know." Pretending nonchalance, she gestured for him to follow her. "Come on. Maybe you can look at it and tell me."

Suddenly a hand closed around her elbow. "I don't think so."

Jane shot him a belligerent look. "What are you doing? I need you upstairs."

"We're not going up there, Jane." His voice was cold as he pressed his gun into her back. "Now, let's go outside or I'll shoot you right here. Then I'll find the prince, and I'll blow his brains out, too."

"Why are you doing this?" Jane shrieked as he shoved her ahead of him toward the exit.

"Oh, Jane, don't play dumb. Money buys everything."

A sob caught in her throat as she stumbled through the back door. Knowing she was trapped, she slid one hand inside her purse, and slowly hit the button to redial Stefan. "Ralph, don't throw away your career "

"My career is already in the crapper, Jane." He pushed her toward one of the crime scene vans and yanked open the door. "Besides, the money we get paid…hell, it's nothing compared to what I got for doing this. I can retire for life."

Jane dug in her heels. "Let's go back inside, talk about this. Running won't help."

"Shut up, Jane." He raised the gun and slammed the butt of it against her head. Pain sliced through her as he shoved her in the van.

STEFAN HAD JUST LEFT Osgood's empty office when his cell phone buzzed. His heart clenched with panic when he heard the scream.

Osgood had Jane.

Blast it.

Taking off at a dead run, he raced down the

steps, yelling for security as he exited the stairwell and ran outside. He didn't spot Osgood or Jane so he ran around the side of the building to the back just in time to see Osgood climb in the crime scene van, gun the engine and speed away.

A security guard rushed up looking harried. "What's going on?"

"Osgood kidnapped Jane Cameron at gunpoint. Alert the sheriff to look for a white van from your office. I am going after them myself."

Not waiting for a response, he jogged around to the parking lot where Jane had parked. He fumbled to open the door, then realized she had the keys in her purse and the van was locked.

Desperate, he ran from car to car searching for one that was unlocked. On the fifth try, he found an unlocked, beat-up Chevy and jumped inside. A second later, he'd hotwired the vehicle and sped into the street.

He raced along the main road from Dumont, his eyes scanning each alley for the van. A few streets down from the main highway out of town, he spotted it barreling in the opposite direction.

Swinging the car around, he hit the gas and prayed he could catch up. Clenching the steering wheel with a white-knuckled grip, he wove around morning traffic, veering down side streets to avoid being seen and following at a distance.

The peaceful wilderness with its cattle grazing and wild horses roaming suddenly seemed ominous, an endless arena of places to hide. What had Osgood done to Jane before he'd put her in the van?

Had he shot her? Was he driving out in the wilderness to bury her so she would never be found?

No…he couldn't let his thoughts stray there…

Several miles on the outskirts of town, the van gained speed, tires screeching as it rounded a curve and veered onto a dirt drive. Stefan slowed and waited several seconds before following, careful again not to be seen tailing the van.

The car bounced over the rough ridges and potholes in the dirt road, the plush farmland giving way to natural desert with boulders and rocks dotting the landscape.

Vultures soared above, and birds of prey screeched and soared along the scrub brush. He punched in Edilio's number.

"Prince Stefan, where are you?" Edilio asked.

Stefan filled him on everything that had happened. "I'm following Osgood now. He has Jane and is armed."

"Prince, you should not be there by yourself. Please, I insist you wait and let the security team handle this matter."

Dust spewed from the van ahead, and he realized the van was stopping, so he parked to the side beneath a cluster of trees. "I have pulled over, Edilio, but I cannot wait. This man knows he has been caught, and he will kill Jane."

"But, Prince, your country, your people, they are depending on you."

To hell with that. Jane needed him now. Stefan inched the Chevy's door open, wincing as the rusty hinges squeaked. "What kind of leader would I be if I watched an innocent woman die just to protect myself?"

"Sir, please, do not jeopardize your life."

"Call the sheriff and give them my location," Stefan said. "Then get out here in case I need backup."

Slowly closing the car door, he silently cursed that he had no weapon. He should have insisted on being armed when the first threat had come.

Instead, now he had only his wits and his fists.

But he had used those before and survived in the military and he would do so now.

Crouching low, he ducked behind the bushes lining the dirt road, inching his way toward the place where Osgood had stopped. An ocelot sauntered across in front of him and he paused, letting it pass.

Ahead he spotted tall bushes, dried brush, a deserted area, then an indentation in the ground with boards propped up against an opening.

An old deserted mine.

Inching closer, he heard Osgood cursing and saw him drag the boards away from the opening and throw them aside. Wiping sweat from his brow, he lumbered back to the van, opened the back and removed a duffel bag.

Stefan gritted his teeth. What was inside?

He craned his neck, listening for Jane, for a scream, any sign she was alive.

But only the quiet hiss of insects, animals skittering and the wind buzzing through the dry bushes echoed back.

Osgood returned to the van, opened the side door, then a second later, he dragged Jane out and threw her over his shoulder. She was pale. Limp. Completely dead weight.

Panic blended with fury as he struggled to see if she was breathing. Her arms dangled beside

Osgood's side as he hauled her to the mine and placed her at the mouth.

Then he laid her down, and Stefan choked on his own breath. Osgood had strapped a bomb around Jane's chest.

Terror momentarily immobilized him. The gods. He could not lose Jane now.

Forcing deep breaths into his lungs to calm his raging heart, he moved forward slowly, forcing his footfalls to be light.

Pebbles skittered beneath his feet though, and Osgood pivoted, searching the area with his eyes. Stefan darted behind a bush to hide just in time. He held his breath as Osgood slowly scanned the area, then finally decided he was safe.

The man was wrong.

Stefan was going to kill him for hurting Jane. But he had to remove the bomb first.

Osgood stooped and opened the duffel bag, then began to unload the contents and Stefan's panic rose.

The timing device for the explosives.

One wrong move and Jane would be gone…

Chapter Fifteen

Stefan eased his way toward the mouth of the mine, hiding behind the bushes until he was only a foot away from Osgood.

The blasted investigator had already set the timer for the bomb!

Rage knotted every muscle in his body, heightening his adrenaline. He lunged toward Osgood and pounced on the man's back. Osgood yelped and jerked his head sideways, aiming his gun upward.

"You damn bastard," Osgood snarled.

Stefan hit the cop's wrist and the gun fell to the ground. Then he yanked Osgood into a chokehold.

But the bully had more strength than Stefan realized and combated his attack with a blow to his abdomen, forcing Stefan's hold to loosen. They fell to the ground, rolling and tumbling, trading blows. Osgood managed to punch Stefan in the nose and blood spurted, but the attack only fueled Stefan's anger.

"You tried to kill Jane," Stefan growled. "But you will not win."

Osgood laughed bitterly. "I'm going to kill you both."

Another fist landed in Stefan's chest then Osgood reached for the gun. Stefan grunted and clawed the dirt for the weapon himself, clasping Osgood's hands just as the man retrieved the weapon. Again they fought for it, but Stefan was determined to stop the bastard. Gritting his teeth, he twisted Osgood's wrist until the bone cracked.

The gun fired, the bullet striking Osgood in the shoulder, and he jerked in pain. The gun sailed from his hands and Stefan took advantage of the moment to pin Osgood down. But Osgood managed to grab a rock with his uninjured arm and swung it up toward Stefan's head.

Stefan dodged the blow, yet the sound of the bomb ticking away echoed from the mine. He had to hurry.

Osgood used his bulk to try to buck Stefan off of him, but Stefan tightened his legs around the man's body, and rammed one fist into Osgood's injured shoulder. Osgood groaned, but swung the rock again.

Stefan caught it just before it connected with his temple and pried it from the man's fingers, then slammed it against Osgood's head. Osgood grunted, his eyes widening then dulling as he passed out.

The ticking reverberated in his head again, faster, faster, faster...

Stefan jumped off of Osgood, kicked the gun out of the way, then ran toward Jane.

A TICKING SOUND ECHOED in Jane's head, drawing her out of the darkness. But when she opened her eyes, she had to squint. The smell of dirt, gunpowder, oil and her own fear surrounded her.

She sucked in a breath, slowly looking down at the bomb attached to her chest. Explosives were wired to a vest, the ticking sound she'd heard moments ago signaling the timer.

Dear God. She was going to die.

Stefan...where was he?

"Jane!"

His voice filtered through the haze of her terror, and she glanced up to see his shadow at the opening to the mine a few inches away. "Stefan, run, he's wired explosives to my chest."

"I am going to get you out of there," Stefan

said in that authoritarian voice that brooked no argument. "Just be very still, Jane."

Her chest rose and fell with a tremulous breath, and she forced herself to lie perfectly still when she wanted to jerk at the vest, tear it off and run herself.

"There's a timing device out here," Stefan said. "I am going to attempt to disarm it."

"No, just get out of here," Jane cried. "It's too dangerous."

Stefan ran to her, knelt and cupped her face in his hands. "Jane, I am not leaving you. Trust me to save you."

A sob caught in her throat. "I do trust you. But I don't want you to die."

"I do not wish that, either," he said with a half smile. "And I will not let you die, either."

She nodded, striving for bravery when she felt as if she was falling apart.

Stefan kissed her quickly, then ran back to the timing device. She forced herself to take shallow breaths, struggling not to fidget or do anything that might trigger the mechanism.

Stefan muttered something to himself about the wires, then the timer. Long, angst-filled seconds passed, dragging into an eternity. The ticking grew louder, pounding in her head. Faster. Faster.

Faster.

The bomb was going to go off any second and they would both be dead.

Stefan suddenly raced back inside. "I am sorry, I cannot diffuse the bomb."

Cold fear pressed against Jane's heart. Then acceptance. She lifted her hand to Stefan's cheek and felt a tear run down her own. "Then go. Save yourself. Your country needs you, Stefan."

Stefan's jaw clamped tight. "I do not intend to leave you, Jane."

"But, Stefan—"

"Be quiet, Jane." His angry hiss forced her to clamp her lips shut.

Then he pulled a knife from his pocket and began to rip at the bindings of the vest.

"Stefan," she whispered. "There's no time."

"I said be quiet." His hands shook as he sawed at the heavy ropes and straps. Her own body trembled as one then another strap gave way. When all were cut, he gripped her arms.

"Now, we're going to do this slowly, Jane."

"Stefan…"

"Shh, love, trust me."

She nodded, although she felt the tugging of the vest, the weight of the explosives, the heat that she knew it would give off.

No, she wouldn't feel the heat. It would all

happen too fast. They would both be blown to smithereens, their body parts scattered. The CSIs would have a field day.

Osgood…

He had done this.

"Where is he? Osgood?"

"Outside, shot, unconscious," Stefan said as he slowly lifted her to a sitting position. She clutched his arms for support until she could steady herself.

"You are doing well," he murmured. "Very good, my Jane. Now we shall extract one arm at a time. Let me know when you are ready."

The ticking seemed to escalate. It was beating now like a drum, so loud her ears ached with the sound.

Her gaze met his, and emotions flickered in his dark eyes. Fear mingled with a confidence that spoke of his military training. And something else—love?

He'd asked her to trust him and she did.

A calmness swept over her, and she nodded. "Let's do it."

He gave her a smile of encouragement, then slowly helped her ease one arm from the vest, then the other. She trembled again as he gently gripped the vest in his hands, then placed it on the earth below her.

Then he stood, swept her up in his arms and ran toward the exit. Just as they made it through the opening, a pop sounded.

Stefan took off at a dead run and dove toward the bushes for cover just as the bomb exploded. Fire, dirt and rocks spewed in all directions, sailing through the air and raining down as the mine collapsed in a thunderous roar.

Jane tasted dirt, felt brush scratching her skin, felt the weight of Stefan as he protected her from the worst, rolling her beneath him and shielding her with his body.

STEFAN HUGGED JANE to him, his heart drumming in his chest. He had almost lost her.

Because of Osgood.

The man who'd threatened Hector and his family. The man who might know where they were being held.

He had to question the man and force him to talk.

Tilting his head back, he stared at Jane, needing to know she was all right. "Are you hurt, Jane?"

Jane shook her head and gripped his arms. "No, are you?"

"I'm fine." He pulled back enough to examine her. "Are you sure you weren't injured?"

"I'm sure, Stefan. You took the worst of the fall." Jane stroked his hair from his forehead in a tender gesture that made him want to wrap his arms around her and never let her go.

Sirens wailed signaling the sheriff's arrival, dust swirling from the train of vehicles barreling up the road. Stefan reluctantly released Jane and stood.

"Osgood may know where Hector's family is being held."

Jane nodded, accepted his extended hand, and he helped her stand. She brushed off her clothes, and he turned and strode toward Osgood. The man was lying amongst the rubble, but just as Stefan reached him, he noticed Osgood's hand clenching the gun. Somehow he'd managed to crawl to it before the bomb had exploded.

Blood seeped from Osgood's shoulder wound, and a deep gash marred his forehead, blood running down his cheeks. The siren wailed closer, the sheriff's SUV careening toward them, an ambulance on its tail.

"You ain't gonna take me in," Osgood choked out.

Stefan held up his hand in an effort to persuade the man to lower the gun. "The sheriff is here, my security is coming. There is no way you will escape now." He stepped closer. "Just tell me where Hector's family is, who has them," Stefan ground out. "If you cooperate, I shall see that your police understand that you helped me."

Osgood coughed, blood leaking into his eye. He tried to swipe at it, but his injured hand hung limply.

Behind him the sheriff's SUV screeched to a halt, then another vehicle. He heard footsteps crunching, voices. The sheriff's. A deputy.

Edilio's.

"Stefan," Edilio said. "Come back, let us handle this matter."

"I know you did not mastermind this plot. Tell me who is holding Hector's family hostage," Stefan pressed. "Who was behind the attack on Amir and me?"

Sweat beaded on Osgood's forehead as he raised the weapon. His hand jerked. "Your enemies are closer than you think."

Osgood started to pull the trigger, but Stefan lurched forward to grab it. In that split second, Osgood swung the gun toward his own head and fired.

Jane screamed, and Stefan staggered backward in shock as blood and brain matter spewed.

Their best lead as to who orchestrated the attacks had just died.

Now how would they find out where Hector's family was and who was behind the attacks?

THE DISTRESS on Stefan's face pained Jane. She wanted to assuage his worries, but she felt as if she'd failed him as well.

Her own boss had been part of the conspiracy against him, and she'd had no idea of his complicity. She hadn't even suspected the bastard.

How could she have been so clueless?

Time passed in a horrific blur as she and Stefan explained to the sheriff what had happened. Edilio kept giving her sharp looks as if he blamed her for this mess, and she couldn't argue the point.

If she hadn't fallen for the prince and had spent more time with Osgood, maybe she would have detected his deception sooner. Then she could have saved Hector and his family from having their lives threatened.

"Whose car is this?" Sheriff Wolf gestured toward the beat-up Chevy.

Stefan's face was riddled with turmoil. "I am afraid I committed a crime. I stole it when I saw Osgood leaving with Jane."

Jane's heart clenched. He had done nothing but save her, and she still had not solved the case.

Stefan held out his hands, wrists together.

"If you must do an American arrest now, I surrender."

Sheriff Wolf shook his head. "Under the circumstances, Prince Stefan, we'll let it go. I'll make certain the owner understands that it was an extreme emergency and that his vehicle was used in the apprehension of a felon."

"I will compensate him for the vehicle monetarily," Stefan offered.

Sheriff Wolf shrugged. "That car isn't worth much. But I'll let you know if there's a problem with the owner."

Stefan nodded and Edilio gestured toward his vehicle. "I will escort you back to the resort now, Prince Stefan."

Stefan glanced at Jane. "We will also escort Miss Cameron."

"I'd prefer to wait until Osgood's body is removed and we retrieve his phone," Jane said. "It might offer some leads as to who masterminded the attacks."

Stefan nodded, and they waited silently while a crew lifted the pipes one by one and loaded Osgood on a stretcher. Jane insisted things be done by the book, so crime scene photos were taken and forensics collected. Her assistant Tomas found Osgood's phone and bagged it to transport to the lab for analysis.

Hours later, when it was time to go, Edilio gave her another disapproving look, but seemed hesitant to argue with Stefan so gestured for her to lead the way toward his dark sedan. A driver was waiting, and she and Stefan slipped into the backseat.

The ride was riddled with tension. Jane twisted her hands in her lap, aching to make things right for Stefan. He stared out the window, his jaw set, his posture rigid as if reliving the scene with Osgood in his mind.

When they arrived, Stefan climbed out, and Jane followed, knowing she should go home. But she needed to speak her mind.

"Stefan, I'm so sorry about Osgood." Her voice cracked. "I should have picked up on his behavior, on his betrayal sooner." The turmoil in his eyes made her shiver. "I know you must hate me."

"Jane…" Stefan paused, body rigid.

"Prince," Edilio cut in. "Would you like for our driver to escort Miss Cameron home while I secure you in your private quarters?"

Stefan gave him a dark look. "No. Miss Cameron stays with me until we discover who is behind these attacks."

"Stefan," Jane whispered, shocked.

"I will not argue this matter," Stefan said

sharply. He closed his fingers around her arm. Edilio frowned but escorted them to Stefan's suite.

As soon as they stepped inside, Stefan dismissed Edilio, then he turned to her. Jane trembled, expecting his wrath.

His look was so dark, so unreadable that for a moment fear trickled through her. Then he jerked her to him, and her pulse clamored.

But instead of shouting at her, he fused his mouth with hers and kissed her so hungrily that her legs buckled.

Chapter Sixteen

Their lovemaking was wild, erotic, frightening, raw, passionate, full of need and fear and tender caresses. Nothing like Jane had ever known. More wonderful than anything she could have imagined.

And everything she had ever wanted.

Exhausted from days without sleep, she closed her eyes, snuggled into his arms and fell asleep dreaming about staying with him forever. About marriage and babies and a long life as Stefan's wife.

But when she awakened, the sun was starting to peak in the morning sky, and Stefan had left the bed.

She slipped on his shirt, then stood and searched for him in the suite, but he was talking in a hushed voice on his cell phone. He had dragged on slacks, but they hung loosely over his muscular hips. She allowed herself a moment to savor the sight of his bronzed chest and sculpted body.

Then he mentioned something about Osgood, and her mind raced back to the case. She needed to search his house, his computer, his desk and see if she could find a link to whoever had taken Hector's family hostage.

Needing caffeine first, she stepped back into the living area to make a pot of coffee and flipped on the television set. A folder with layouts of Stefan's environmental plan lay on the table. She opened it and skimmed through the details while the coffee brewed.

The sound of Danny Harold's voice from the television caught her attention.

"This is Danny Harold. I'm here now with a local ranch family the McGuires from the Seven M Ranch nearby. Mr. McGuire, tell us how you feel about the dignitaries visiting the Wind River Ranch and Resort."

"My name is Clay," the father of the bunch said. "I've ranched in Wyoming all my life. I don't like these foreigners coming in trying to do business here, and I sure as heck don't trust 'em. Why, they've already caused one bombing in these parts."

Jane shook her head, half listening, half ignoring the man's remarks. She was impressed with Stefan's plan and excited at the possibility that Wyoming could profit financially from their oil resources while being environmentally conscious.

McGuire had no idea the good the summit could do both for peace relations and for Wyoming itself.

As soon as the interview with McGuire ended, the camera switched to an interview with Sheriff Wolf. He looked uncomfortable in front of the camera and exhausted. No doubt he'd been up half the night sorting out the mess with Osgood's suicide.

"Sheriff," Harold asked. "Is it true that one of your CSI agents was killed last night in the line of duty?"

Sheriff Wolf gave Harold a cool look. "It is true that one of our CSI agents lost his life, but I cannot release details surrounding the circumstances just yet. There is an ongoing investigation into the matter—"

"But isn't it true that Mr. Osgood was working with some sort of terrorist group that caused the bombing of the limousine carrying one of the dignitaries? And that Osgood kidnapped one of your other agents and tried to kill her and Prince Stefan?"

Jane gasped. Where in the world was Harold getting his information?

Sheriff Wolf's jaw clamped so tightly a vein throbbed in his neck. "As I said, I cannot discuss the details of an ongoing investigation. I will hold a press conference when we have more to share."

With that comment, Sheriff Wolf walked away. The camera panned back to Harold who was grinning like a Cheshire cat. Jane poured herself a cup of coffee and was just about to take a sip when Harold continued, and a photograph of Stefan appeared on the screen.

"Speaking of Prince Stefan," Harold continued. "Sources have revealed that the Prince is due to marry once he returns to his country of Kyros."

Jane choked on the coffee, burned her tongue and splashed it on her hand. The hot sting was nothing, though, compared to the sharp pain in her chest.

"According to King Maximes, Stefan's father, the prince will wed King Nazim's daughter, Princess Daria, in a traditional ceremony uniting both their lives and their countries…"

"No, this cannot be…" Stefan murmured behind her. "That…was not supposed to air."

Jane swung around and saw Stefan staring at the screen in stunned disbelief.

Hurt raised her defenses. "What?" Jane asked in a thick voice. "You didn't want the American women to know you were engaged to a princess back home?"

STEFAN SWALLOWED, bile rising to his throat. How had this American news reporter heard of Daria and his father's plans?

He swung his gaze back to Jane and saw the hurt in her eyes, and his stomach rose to his throat. "Jane, I do not know how this information made it to your press."

Her lips compressed into a thin line. "Because you wanted your engagement kept private?"

"No, that is not it." He reached for her to explain, but she spun away and grabbed her clothes then dashed into the bathroom.

He raced after her and knocked on the door. "Please, Jane, I must explain. The engagement—"

"No need to explain!" Jane shouted through the closed door.

A second later, the door flew open, and Jane elbowed past him.

"Jane, please listen," Stefan said, panic rising in his chest. "I can explain. This marriage…my father, he wants it, but—"

Jane threw her shoulder bag over her arm. "Stop, Stefan. You don't owe me an explanation."

"But I do. We…us—"

"There is no us, Stefan," Jane said matter-of-factly. "You had your American fling, I got to sleep with a prince." She strode toward the door, then pivoted and lifted her chin in that defiant way that intrigued and infuriated him at the same time. "We both know that anything more than a romp in the hay wasn't in our future. Now, I need to search Osgood's computer. Maybe there's information on it that will lead us to Hector's family."

Jane's declaration reminded him that Hector's family was still missing. Last night he'd let Jane's sultry body sidetrack him. What kind of leader was he going to be if bedding a woman took priority over a crisis?

Stefan scanned the room for his shirt then remembered that Jane had been wearing it and had discarded it in the bathroom. And the gods, she had looked so sexy in it… "Let me finish dressing. I will go with you."

"No," Jane snapped. "Stay here with your security team. This is my job. You'll only be in the way."

Hurt stabbed at him, and he swallowed hard, struggling over a response. But Jane didn't give him time to reply. She darted out the door and disappeared down the hallway before he could stop her.

He dug through his clothes for a shirt, but his cell phone buzzed. He checked the number. Efraim.

His friends needed to be updated on the events of the night before, and he owed them the truth, not Danny Harold's version, so he connected the call. "Stefan speaking."

"Stefan, what is going on? Antoine and Sebastian and I heard a news report about an attack last night against you and Ms. Cameron."

"Meet me in the conference room in fifteen minutes and I will explain." He disconnected, then hurried to shower.

Jane was doing her job now. Osgood was dead, so hopefully she would be safe. And he needed the answers she could provide with her expertise.

It was time for him to act like a prince and do his job as well.

Perhaps he should even consider marrying Daria as his father had insisted. A marriage with her would be loveless, but it would solve his country's immediate problems and stop this vicious cycle of violence that this trip had caused.

After all, anyone he married might be in danger in the future.

But could he relinquish his dreams, his plans, his goals and…his love? Would that not be allowing these terrorists to win?

Anger thrummed through him as he punched in his brother's number. He intended to find out exactly who was responsible for leaking the story about Daria. The servant answered, but he asked to be put through immediately.

"Thaddeus, did you tell the press that I was going to marry Daria?"

His brother hesitated. "Yes. Father is growing more ill, Stefan, and he needs to know Kyros is secure before he passes. You need to step up and do your duty."

"I am doing my duty," Stefan bit out. "But if I lead Kyros, I will lead it in my own way. And that means bringing it into the twenty-first century, not agreeing to an arranged marriage for business purposes."

"There are far worse things," Thaddeus said.

He could think of nothing worse than marrying drab Daria when his heart belonged with beautiful Jane Cameron. "As I said, I have my own plans for Kyros."

His brother scoffed. "Plans? Look what a

mess you have made in America. You, a prince, chasing down pedestrian police officers and engaging in fistfights."

Stefan frowned. "How do you know of my actions?"

"Your security team does coordinate with our men here, Stefan. Now give up this ridiculous summit and come home and make Father happy. Kyros needs to be maintained as the lovely resort it is, not become another oil drilling catastrophe that will invite more distress and crime in the Middle East."

Stefan had to count to ten to maintain his patience. He glanced at his clock and realized his friends would be waiting, and he did not want to waste another moment arguing with his idiotic brother.

"Just tell Julius to find Hector's family, and to alert me as soon as he does. I must know that they are unharmed."

Without giving his brother time to argue again, he disconnected the call.

Body tense with frustration, he made quick work of dressing, then exited the room. Edilio was standing guard outside his door and escorted him down the hall.

"My men say Jarryd has been vocal in

opposing the summit. They have detained him for questioning but so far have found no link to him, and he denies knowledge of the Perro kidnapping."

"Good, maybe we'll make some headway," Stefan said. He entered the conference room where Efraim, Antoine and Sebastian all stood anxiously waiting. Fahad had also joined them, both as head of security and coordinator for the individual teams.

"Stefan, are you all right?" Efraim asked, his face etched with worry.

"Yes." Stefan motioned for them to take a seat, and he explained about Osgood's betrayal and the coercion techniques he'd used against Hector. "Osgood was working with a sniper from the Russian mob, and apparently helped orchestrate the threat to Hector's family. But someone else masterminded the plot."

"Who?" Antoine asked.

"I do not know yet." Stefan's throat went dry. "My people in Kyros are searching for the Perro family now. When they are found, perhaps they can tell us more."

"What can we do?" Sebastian drummed his hands on the table. "I am most disgusted sitting here doing nothing while Amir is in need of our help."

"I agree," Antoine said. "We must form a plan of action."

Stefan ran a hand over the back of his neck. "We definitely cannot trust the local police."

"Even this Sheriff Wolf?" Efraim asked.

Stefan considered the question. "I believe he is above board." He paused. "However, we must rely on our own security teams. Have your agents uncovered any suspects from your list of enemies?" Stefan asked.

"We have not determined anyone specific as of yet," Fahad said. "But trust me, we are diligently pursuing every possible lead."

"Good. Tell them to keep searching," Stefan said.

"Is it true that you have agreed to marry Daria?" Efraim asked.

So they had seen that news segment as well. Damn Thaddeus.

Stefan frowned. If he went through with the marriage, it meant relinquishing his own plans for Kyros. And he was not ready to accept defeat.

"No, I have already spoken with my brother,

and I will speak to Father shortly." He only prayed the news did not upset his father to the point that his condition worsened.

Stefan's phone buzzed again, and he glanced down at the display screen. Jane.

Hoping she'd called to apologize for leaving and that she wished to talk, he connected the call.

"Stefan, it's Jane."

"Yes?"

"Computer crimes reviewed Osgood's phone records again, and there's another number here that we're questioning. The number is for someone in Kyros."

Stefan stepped aside for a moment. Jarryd? "Yes, what is this number?"

Jane recited the number and Stefan's blood began to boil.

"If you don't recognize it," Jane said, "perhaps Edilio or Fahad can look into it."

Stefan hissed through clenched teeth. "I recognize it."

A heartbeat of silence followed. "Who does it belong to?"

Stefan lowered his head into his hands, sickened at the thought that another person close to him, someone else he trusted, might be involved in this conspiracy, that he might actually want him dead. That he could have killed innocents.

"Stefan?" Jane asked. "You know who it is?"

"Yes." Stefan's throat felt thick. But it was not Jarryd. "It belongs to my brother, Thaddeus."

JANE'S HEART BLED at the anguish in Stefan's reply. His brother had contacted Osgood. And not just once, more than once.

Which suggested that his brother might have been behind Hector's family's disappearance and the attacks on Stefan and Jane.

"I must go, Jane," Stefan said curtly. "I will handle this matter immediately."

"Stefan, please let me—"

"Thank you," he said. "You were right. You are good at your job."

She opened her mouth to respond, but the phone went dead.

Jane squeezed the handset, her emotions in turmoil. First, Hector had set him up, then he'd learned that he had been coerced.

Now to discover that his own brother might have orchestrated the attacks.

Memories bombarded her. Stefan risking his life to save her. Stefan kissing her for the first time. The passionate way he'd held her in the night. The hungry way he'd made love to her as if she was the only woman in the world. The sultry way he'd murmured her name as if she was beautiful, as if their lovemaking meant something special to him as it had to her.

When she'd left his room this morning, she'd raced home and tried to shower his scent off of her, but nothing could erase those memories from her mind. Or the memory of hearing that he was marrying another woman.

She retrieved her shoulder bag and headed for the door.

She was the biggest kind of fool. She had sworn she wouldn't fawn all over the royals like the teenage girls, yet the moment Stefan had looked at her, she'd been lost.

Even if he had wanted her for more than a night of fun, she could never be with him. She would lose herself if she did.

Tomas poked his head in the door. "Jane?"

Reality dragged her from her tumultuous thoughts. "What is it, Tomas?"

"I found something else on Osgood's phone."

Jane dropped her purse and crossed the distance to review the printout in his hand.

Tomas pointed to an exchange between Osgood and an anonymous source. "Look at this one."

Her breath caught in her chest as she read the message.

Bomb failed. Intended for all the coalition. Move to Plan B.

Chapter Seventeen

"What's wrong, Stefan?" Efraim asked.

Stefan swallowed back bile. "I have a possible lead."

"About Amir?"

"I am not sure." Although perhaps his brother had something to do with that as well. Perhaps the bomb had been meant for him, not Amir, all along. Or his brother had decided killing all of them was worth it as long as Stefan died.

"It is about Osgood," he said, "perhaps a connection to whoever is holding Hector's family hostage."

"What can we do?" Efraim asked.

"Let me make a call," Stefan said. "Then I will update you."

Efraim returned to the group, and Stefan stepped aside and informed Edilio of the news.

"Please phone Julius and ask him to send a team to interrogate my brother," Stefan said.

Edilio's brow shot up. "Prince, you want Thaddeus interrogated?"

Stefan realized Edilio was waiting to see if Stefan would authorize severe interrogation tactics if needed.

"Yes." Stefan forced a calmness to his voice and tried to obliterate images of him and his brother playing together as children from his mind. Of the two of them running through the backyard and swimming in the Mediterranean. Of playful swordfights and fishing expeditions and brawls over girls in school.

If Thaddeus had Benito killed and orchestrated these attacks, he was no longer the brother Stefan had known.

"We must find out if he was complicit in the kidnapping of Hector's family and where they are." Stefan lowered his voice. "Set up a satellite feed. I wish to watch my brother's reaction when your men question him."

Edilio stared at him now with a worried look. "Are you certain, Prince?

"Yes," Stefan said in his most commanding voice. "I will be able to discern if my brother is lying. Now, set it up."

His heart hardened. If Thaddeus was guilty, he would order whatever means necessary to unearth the truth.

JANE SPED TOWARD the resort, debating whether to call first, but Stefan had asked her not to trust anyone, and now she understood his reasoning. Besides, she wanted to relay the disturbing text in person so he could warn the other royals.

Plan B. What the hell was Plan B?

Fear made her press the gas pedal to the floor, and she zipped past the ranches and wilderness toward the resort and spa, her heart in her throat as she remembered making love with Stefan.

And then she'd seen that picture of Princess Daria.

An exotic creature who would not only look beautiful on Stefan's arm, but one who would be his wife. She would bear his children. Share his thoughts, his plans for his country, his bed, his life…

Princess Daria would be the perfect wife and would fit into Stefan's world.

Jane would not.

She belonged here with the cows and wilderness and her crime scenes.

Tears trickled down her cheeks, a sob escaping her throat. She swiped at them, angry at herself for relenting to his charms.

And for falling in love with the man.

Yes, plain Jane had fallen hopelessly in love with a prince.

A man engaged to another woman, one who would leave her behind with heavenly memories of lying in his bed, sated and aching for more.

A man who had ruined her for being with someone else because no other man in the world could ever complete her the way Stefan had.

Stop it, Jane. You're survived alone all these years. You'll survive when he leaves and marries the princess.

Because a princess was the one thing a plain Jane could never be.

The resort slid into view, a magnificent spectacle in the midst of the wild, and Jane veered into the drive, drying her tears with the back of her hand.

This visit concerned work and work only. The royals needed to know they were still in danger, that someone else was plotting to kill them and stop the COIN compact.

She patted her shoulder bag, one hand slipping over her gun. Stefan had been betrayed by Hector, and she had been betrayed by her own boss.

She'd do anything she had to do to protect Stefan, even though he would leave her in the end.

She swung the SUV into a parking place, jumped out and hurried toward Stefan's cottage.

When she arrived, a security guard was staked outside.

She flashed her ID. "I need to see Prince Stefan," Jane said.

"He's in the conference room with the COIN members, ma'am."

She pivoted and raced along the garden walkway to the main resort building, then hurried inside. Security guards for the royals seemed to be everywhere, but she showed them her ID, and they let her pass.

When she arrived at the conference room, she spoke to Fahad. "I need to see Stefan and the COIN members. It's urgent."

"Prince Stefan is in the adjoining office. The others are inside waiting for him."

She hesitated. She could just talk to the others, let them pass the word to Stefan. But that was cowardly, and Jane Cameron was no coward. "I'll see Prince Stefan first."

Fahad gave her an intimidating look, and for a moment, a frisson of fear traipsed up her spine. But another guard walked by, and he led her to the office.

She spotted Edilio beside Stefan acting as a buffer/guard and strode over to them. Stefan was standing, his posture rigid, his face a stern mask as he watched some kind of live video feed.

"Thaddeus, you did this," Stefan said. You tried to kill me and you had Hector's family kidnapped."

Jane froze, her eyes glued to the screen where a man was strapped to a chair in a small dingy room. Two soldiers flanked him, their faces earnest, weapons in their hands. The man's face was bloody, his clothes torn and soaked in blood as well as if he'd been beaten to within an inch of his life.

It was Stefan's brother. She'd seen his photograph in the exposé about Stefan that had aired before the royals had arrived.

"You should have just agreed to marry Daria," Thaddeus bellowed. "Then I would not have been forced to take the measures that I did."

Stefan clenched the desk edge with a white-knuckled grip, his face raw with pain and rage. "And you should have never told the press that that marriage was on," Stefan said.

Thaddeus spit blood onto the scarred floor. "But Daria would be best for you, Stefan, and for our country. You will ruin Kyros with your plans."

"I cannot marry Daria when my heart is with someone else," Stefan said between clenched teeth.

Jane gasped, and Stefan suddenly glanced

up as if he realized she was there. Their gazes locked, and the anguish and grief of his brother's betrayal gleamed in his eyes, nearly bringing her to her knees.

"AND WHO IS THIS in your heart?" Thaddeus yelled. "Some American whore you have bedded while you are there selling out our country?"

Stefan jerked his gaze from Jane. He wanted to take her in his arms, promise her forever, apologize for the way she'd learned about Daria, shield her from this scene with his brother. And he wanted to beat his brother himself for his vile words.

But he had to maintain control.

Still, if he had a chance for a future with Jane, she had to see him for who he was.

For the kind of man it took to be the leader he was born to be.

He would not back down from a fight.

So he straightened and forced his voice to a commanding tone, reining in his emotions. "Who I marry is not your concern," Stefan said. "I am the leader of Kyros now, and I will rule as I choose just as I will marry whom I choose."

"You selfish—"

"Your feelings about me do not matter, brother. The only thing that does is that you have betrayed me. You ordered that bomb that destroyed the limo carrying Amir—"

"I did not order the bomb," Thaddeus shouted. "That was not me."

Stefan swallowed hard. "But the Russian sniper, Hector's family?"

Thaddeus clammed up, then spit again. "Go to hell, Stefan."

One of the soldiers glanced at Stefan, and he nodded, giving a silent order. The soldier swung his baton back and hit Thaddeus across the chest, then his face. Thaddeus cried out, his head jerking as blood spewed from his nose.

Jane wavered beside him, and he shot her an apologetic look, but he couldn't stop now. Hector had been like family and Thaddeus had caused him great suffering.

"Where is Hector's family?" Stefan asked in a lethal tone.

Thaddeus groaned. "Agree not to press charges against me and I will tell you."

"Oh, you will tell me anyway," Stefan said. "And, brother, do not expect to get off after what you have done."

Thaddeus gave Stefan a hate-filled look, and Stefan again gestured to the guard. This time he picked up a hypodermic and waved it in front of Thaddeus' face.

"You know what is in that," Stefan said. "It is the substance we have been experimenting with. Would you like to know what happens to your body once it is injected?"

Jane laid a hand on his shoulder, and he tensed, then glanced at her, expecting to see disgust, but a myriad of emotions swirled in her eyes. Fear was there. But also understanding. Compassion.

And a strength that reminded him of who Jane was. A brave woman who fought for what was right as well. They would make a dynamic pair.

If only Jane could see that.

Another strike and Thaddeus's shout jerked Stefan back to the immediate matter at hand. His lying, despicable brother.

Thaddeus trembled, sweat streaming down his face and neck. "You would not do that to your own brother. You cannot, Stefan. What would Father think?"

Stefan released a weary sigh. "Ah, what will he think when he learns you tried to have me killed? That you hired a sniper who murdered one of our security agents? That you have Hector's family under siege terrorizing them?"

Panic flashed in Thaddeus's eyes, and he jerked at the bindings, but the soldier played his part well and lowered the needle toward Thaddeus' neck.

"Where are they?" Stefan ordered.

"Stop!" Thaddeus cried as the soldier pressed the needle to his throat. "Stop. I will tell you. Hector's family is alive."

The soldier hesitated, waiting on Stefan's orders. "Where are they, Thaddeus?"

Thaddeus was half crying now, tears mingling with the blood on his cheeks. "Two men are holding them in an abandoned warehouse nearby."

Stefan's voice held an icy edge, "Give Julius the location."

Thaddeus nodded, his breath raspy as he gave Julius an address, then Julius ordered his team to check out the information.

Julius addressed Stefan. "What do you want us to do with your brother?"

"Hold him until we verify that Hector's family is released, and that they are all unharmed. And keep pumping him about what happened to Amir. If he ordered that bomb, we need to know."

"And your father?" Julius asked.

Stefan's chest ached. "Please make sure that news of this is not leaked to the press or that it reaches him. His health is too delicate now.

When I am finished here, I will fly home and relay the news myself."

Julius nodded obediently and rushed from the room. Thaddeus dropped his head forward in defeat while the soldiers stood with guns aimed at him if he attempted an escape.

One of the soldiers punched Thaddeus again, pressing him for information on Amir.

"I swear," Thaddeus cried. "I had nothing to do with that bomb. You can beat me to death, but I cannot tell you what I do not know."

They spent another ten minutes interrogating him, but Thaddeus still insisted that he had not orchestrated the bombing.

Jane's breath sounded choppy next to Stefan, yet she refrained from speaking, and so did he.

Finally Stefan gave the order to halt the interrogation. His brother had admitted to several crimes already. If he knew about Amir, he would have broken by now.

Tension vibrated through the room as they waited on Julius to see if Thaddeus had been truthful, if the rescue of the Perros was successful or not.

Sickened by his brother, Stefan paced to the window and stared out. He had come to America to do what he thought was right for Kyros.

Was he making a mistake in defying his father's wishes about marriage? In pushing for the oil mining on Kyros instead of leaving the country as a resort?

Blast it. He wanted it all. Had thought when he'd come to the U.S. with his friends that he could have it all.

He glanced at Jane, but she sank into a chair, hands folded, looking at them, at anything but at him. She must hate him now she'd seen what kind of man lurked below the surface.

But he loved her so.

Was it wrong for him to desire a life with a woman who held his heart instead of a woman who did not love him, a woman who was being forced to marry him for business?

JANE STARED at her hands, willing herself to be strong. She ached to go to Stefan and comfort him, but she didn't think he would welcome it in front of his men.

He was obviously distraught over using physical violence against his brother, and although the images disturbed her, she understood that he had been forced to do so.

His brother was a liar, a man who had ordered Stefan's death. A man who had caused the death of Benito and ordered Hector's family to be held hostage.

Stefan was a good leader, a man of courage, of intelligence, a man who made sacrifices for his own people yet he had values she admired as well.

How could she not have fallen in love with him?

He's not marrying Princess Daria He'd said his heart belonged to someone else.

Her heart skittered, and she tore her gaze from her fingers and glanced up at him. He was watching her with hooded eyes.

What was he thinking? Was there someone else he'd given his heart to, someone in Kyros?

Or could he possibly love her?

Chapter Eighteen

Minutes stretched into hours as Stefan waited on news about the Perros. Stefan paced, constantly glaring at his brother who was sweating profusely. When had his brother grown so bitter and selfish? When had he changed into a man who would hurt family and friends?

Finally Julius phoned.

Stefan gritted his teeth. "Did you find them?"

"Yes," Julius said. "The Perros were frightened, but they are all alive and unharmed, and my men have arrested the men watching them."

Stefan dropped his head into his hands, trembling in relief. "Thank God. Assign guards to watch the family until the situation here is resolved, and you receive word from me. I want them to rest assured that they are no longer in danger."

He turned to Edilio. "Please go inform Hector. And let him talk to his family."

He glanced at Jane and saw the relief on her face as well. But he still had to deal with Thaddeus.

He addressed the soldiers standing guard over his brother. "The Perros are safe."

"Now you can let me go," Thaddeus pleaded.

"No, brother. It causes me great suffering to do this, but you have destroyed lives, even taken lives. You must pay for your crimes." Stefan's heart ached as he gestured toward the soldiers. "Arrest him and place him in solitary confinement. But secrecy is of utmost importance. No details of this are to be announced until I speak with my father and Amir is found."

Thaddeus pleaded and begged like a coward, but Stefan did not change his mind. He watched as the soldiers handcuffed his brother and dragged him from the room.

Dread filled his chest as he contemplated how to tell his father. But he still had matters to take care of here first. Locating Amir ranked at the top of the list.

Jane stood and faced him, her expression troubled. "I know that was difficult for you, Prince Stefan."

Hurt mushroomed inside him. "I am no longer Stefan to you?"

Jane blushed as if his words resurrected the intimacy they had once shared.

"You heard me say that I am not to marry Princess Daria," Stefan said. "That that news release was a mistake."

Jane's expression softened. "Yes. But even so, Stefan, we both know that what we had was… just because of the situation, the danger here. That you are a prince. You belong in Kyros leading your people, and I have no place by your side."

Anger threatened to surface. Why must she be so obstinate? "Do you not think that I should have some choice in this matter? That I know best who should stand by my side?"

Jane closed her eyes as if battling her emotions, and he realized she was. For all of her independence and tough veneer, she was afraid of getting hurt. Afraid he would desert her as her mother's lover had.

When she opened her eyes, sadness and resignation darkened the depths. How would he ever convince her he was an honorable man she could trust with her heart?

He could not. Not as long as she saw him as a prince.

Jane cleared her throat. "Stefan, there's

something else. The reason I came here. It's important."

Disappointment hit him like a blow. Obviously it was not to confess her undying love for him.

"Yes, Jane?"

"It has to do with your friends as well. Perhaps I could tell you all at once."

That was Jane. Always doing her job. How could he love and admire her so much and want to shake her at the same time?

"Very well," he said. "Let us go join the others. They are waiting in the conference room."

He started to take her arm, but Jane avoided his touch and plowed ahead of him, leading the way. He watched her delicious hips sway and feared that any closeness they had shared was now lost forever.

A hollowness filled him.

Then fear. Did Jane have bad news about Amir?

JANE RUSHED to the conference room, determined to finish this investigation with her heart intact.

Fahad approached Stefan, his expression stern. "What happened, Prince Stefan?"

Somber, Stefan relayed the latest development, and revealed his brother's involvement.

"Did Thaddeus have information about Amir?" Efraim asked.

Stefan's signet ring bearing the crown twinkled in the light as he scrubbed a hand through his hair, reminding Jane of his position.

"No," Stefan said. "He denies any involvement in the bombing."

"And you believe him?" Prince Antoine asked.

Stefan nodded, then gestured toward Jane. "But Miss Cameron has something of importance to speak with us about."

Jane cleared her throat. "I'm sorry to have to tell you this—"

"Amir is dead?" Efraim staggered backward.

"No," Jane said, realizing his panic. "I don't know where he is, nor do I have any information regarding him in particular."

Stefan narrowed his eyes, obviously confused. "Then what is it, Jane?"

She handed him a printout. "We found a text on CSI Osgood's phone. We haven't determined the source yet, but the message is alarming."

"What does it say?" Efraim asked.

Stefan's face twisted with worry. "That the

bomb was intended for all of us, but failed. That it is time for Plan B."

Worried sighs and murmurs rumbled through the room.

"What is Plan B?" Prince Sebastian asked.

Jane shook her head. "I don't know. When we trace the source of the message, maybe we can find out the answer to that question."

Fahad stepped to the front of the room. "Until then, it is best that each of you remain sequestered inside the resort. I will make your security teams aware of this danger and that you should be monitored around the clock."

"I do not like this," Efraim complained. "We must do something to find Amir ourselves."

"I agree," Prince Antoine said firmly.

Prince Sebastian mumbled agreement. "Each day Amir is missing lessens the chances that we find him alive."

Stefan nodded. "The betrayal by my brother and the local police proves we cannot trust anyone. And I agree that we must find our friend." He glanced at Jane. "But for tonight, Fahad is right. We must lie low and consider our list of enemies, then meet to strategize tomorrow."

The men shook hands in agreement and filed

out. Jane turned to leave, but Stefan caught her arm.

"I do not wish you to go just yet."

"You can't order me around," Jane said, although her voice cracked with emotions. The thought of Stefan still being in danger made her shake in her shoes. She wanted to stay to protect him.

She wanted to run to protect her own heart.

But she couldn't leave him now, not until she knew every threat was resolved. Not until they had found Amir and the person who'd orchestrated the bomb attack.

Chapter Nineteen

Stefan studied his beautiful, stubborn woman. He needed to get her alone, in his arms, in his bed again where he could convince her that she belonged with him. That he loved her and he intended to make her his bride.

A plan struck him, and he made up his mind. "It is not an order, but a request," he said gruffly.

Jane's heart softened. "I will stay to protect you, Stefan, and to finish the investigation."

His mouth thinned. "Very well then. But I meant what I said. Tonight is for rest and regrouping."

"Then you should rest, Stefan. I'll wait here."

"No, meet me in the stables. I have not seen this resort and tonight I wish to."

Jane looked so puzzled that he almost chuckled. "Okay," she said warily. "But I'm just going as your bodyguard."

"My body is yours to do with as you wish," he said with a hint of a smile.

Jane's cheeks pinkened, but she patted her shoulder bag. "All right. I'll follow you to your quarters."

He glanced at his dress clothes. "No, I wish to change first. Edilio will escort me to the stables. Meet me there at dusk."

She gave him a suspicious look, and he bit his lip to keep from laughing aloud. He had perplexed his Jane.

Just wait until she found him in the stables.

He made quick work of enlisting Edilio to help him carry out his plan. His security agent was not pleased, but Stefan reminded him that his job was to safeguard him, not to interfere with how he chose to live his life.

With the help of the Wind River Ranch and Resort staff, his plan came together, and shortly before dusk, Edilio escorted him to the stables to execute his plan. If this did not work, he would have to consult someone who knew more about the complexity of the American woman's mind than himself.

Dreaming of Jane on his arm when he returned to Kyros, with the COIN compact signed, Amir safe and alive, his environmental plan in effect, his country financially sound, and the woman he loved by his side, he stepped into the stable to choose the perfect horses for him and Jane to ride.

After all, he had fantasized about Jane straddling a horse, and this was one fantasy he intended to fulfill tonight.

JANE POKED HER HEAD in to the stables door, her nerves ping-ponging back and forth. Stefan had acted strangely those last few minutes, as if he had something up his sleeve.

What was he up to?

He's not your prince, Jane.

It took her eyes a moment to adjust to the dim interior of the barn, and she realized that some of the lights were turned off. Instantly her suspicions rose, and she removed her gun, moving cautiously inside.

"Stefan?"

No reply.

Perspiration beaded on her neck. "Stefan, are you in here? Are you all right?" She took another step, then heard one of the horses bray.

Then a gruff, low voice. "Back here, Jane."

Frowning, she inched past the first stall, stopping to pat the horse who poked his head out for her attention. The mare across the way kicked, wanted petting as well, but she had to reach Stefan and make sure someone hadn't set a trap.

"Stefan, are you okay?"

"Yes, Jane, now come to the last stall."

Sawdust skidded below her feet as she passed the next few stalls, then she halted when she spotted a cowboy mucking the last stall. "Excuse me, sir, where's Prince Stefan?"

She aimed the gun, ready to shoot in case he attacked.

But the cowboy slowly turned around and reality dawned. The cowboy was Stefan.

A black Stetson shadowed his chiseled face, making him look rugged and mysterious, and so damn sexy that her throat went dry. And that black Western shirt emphasized his broad chest just as the pair of well-worn jeans hugging his lean muscular hips stirred images of the raw man beneath.

"Stefan?" her voice squeaked.

"Yes, Jane, it is me, love."

Love? Her heart melted. "What are you doing?"

"Cleaning the stall. I have chosen two beautiful specimens for us to ride."

"But—"

"Are you going to shoot me or join me?" He quirked his head toward her drawn weapon.

"I…" Her pulse clamored. "I thought this might be a trap."

Laughter gleamed in his eyes, and she realized that in some devious sexual way that it was, although she hadn't exactly figured out what Stefan was up to.

He shrugged, lifted a gloved hand and pushed the gun downward, then led a stallion from the stall. Speechless, she stowed her weapon in her purse and followed him, then stood watching in awe as he saddled up the black horse and a white palomino.

"What are you doing? They have stable hands who would have saddled the horses," Jane said in a weak voice.

Stefan turned to her, his eyes serious and intent. "I am proving to you that I am not a spoiled prince. Well, maybe I am a bit spoiled," he teased. "But I am also fit and capable. I am intelligent, have military experience, can ride a horse as well as your Wyoming cowboys, and I am totally smitten with you, Jane."

Smitten? Had he heard that expression from some ancient American-made movie?

"I know you're intelligent, Stefan. I saw your environmental package. It's brilliant."

He arched a brow, obviously pleased with her compliment. "So perhaps you are smitten with me as well?"

She clamped her teeth over her lower lip. God, she wasn't smitten. She was head over hells in love. In fact, he had both horses literally and figuratively eating out of the palm of his hand, and if he kept talking in that seductive voice and looking at her with those bedroom eyes, she would be, too.

"Stefan…"

A tender smile tilted his lips, and he gestured for her to climb on the palomino. "You do ride, Jane? You are not afraid of horses, too, are you?"

She tensed at the barb, but stuck her chin in the air. "Of course, I ride. And no, I'm not afraid of horses."

He mounted his own horse, and gave her a teasing look. "But horses can be dangerous, Jane. They can throw you then move onto another rider with no remorse."

She frowned. "Why would you say a thing like that?"

At the shadow in his eyes, she realized he knew about her mother.

Of course, he'd researched her past. His security team probably had dossiers on everyone at the ranch and on the police force.

Dammit, she wished he couldn't see through her so well.

Desperate to avoid the conversation, she gave the horse a firm kick and sent him galloping from the barn. Stefan followed, and for the next few minutes, they rode in silence, enjoying the peace and quiet and beauty of the resort.

Antelope and other wild animals roamed freely, cattle grazed inside acres and acres of pasture, and birds flocked to the gardens and numerous birdfeeders scattered throughout the land.

Freshly cut grass, trees, and flowers scented the air while a falcon soared above, graceful and elegant against the sky, and the creek gurgled feeding into the river nearby.

Stefan rode with poise and ease and command of the animal beneath him, just as he did everything else in his life. Her body stirred, hungry for him, heat rippling through her as she watched the gentle way he stroked the horse's neck and murmured appreciation.

Finally he guided his horse to a pond where he slowed, then stopped and climbed off. Jane

followed his lead, and they let the horses rest.
But she felt unsettled, her body humming to life
as Stefan took her hand and coached her to the
pond. To her surprise, a picnic basket sat in the
midst of a blanket, waiting. Stefan must have set
it up earlier.

Jane watched, her nerves skittering with
awareness and anticipation as he uncorked a
bottle of wine, opened it and poured them each
a glass. When he handed it to her, his fingers
brushed hers, igniting a fiery heat through her.

Damn. He was sexy in a suit, and naked, but
dressed in those tight jeans and that Stetson, he
was a tempting sight.

"What are you doing?" Jane asked.

He chuckled and sipped his wine. "Trying to
seduce the woman I love." He quirked a brow.
"Is it working?"

The woman he loved?

His words stirred her innermost feelings, feelings she'd desperately tried to avoid. He couldn't
mean it, that he loved her. He was only caught
up in the moment.

Feeling jittery, she sipped from her own
glass, warmed by the heady taste of the merlot.
"Stefan—"

"Shh. I am not the man your mother married,
and you are not her." He slowly walked toward

her, his eyes intent on her face. "Now that is settled. This is a bottle from my own country of Kyros," he murmured in a sex-laden voice. "There are so many beautiful things there that I wish to show you, Jane. That I wish to share with you."

Jane's heart pitched. "Stefan, this is incredibly romantic, and you look sexy as hell—"

"I am sexy to you?" He tilted his head with a lazy swagger that made her smile in spite of herself.

"Of course you are." She threw her hands up in frustration. "But that's not the point. The point is that I would never fit into your world." She gestured toward herself. "Just look at me. You're a prince. You deserve a princess, someone—"

"I am a prince," he said gruffly. "I cannot change that, Jane." He tilted his Stetson, then gestured toward his body. "But with you, I am just a man."

Jane wet her lips with her tongue. "You're so much more than just a man," she whispered.

"I am a man you like?"

Jane hedged. "Yes."

One brow shot up. "A man you enjoy being with?"

Another smile surfaced against her will. "Yes."

His eyes glinted. "A man who pleasured you well in bed?"

"Stefan," Jane whispered, heat climbing her neck.

"Did I not?" he asked, serious now. "Because if there is something more you wish in the ways of pleasuring you, I am most willing for you to show me." He trailed his fingers down her shoulder to her breast, making her nipples instantly stiffen. "I am a quick learner, Jane."

"Stefan," Jane said, feeling flushed. "You were wonderful. Perfect. But that's not the problem."

"There is no problem, Jane, except in your mind," Stefan said. "I choose who I want," he said earnestly, passionately. "And you, Jane Cameron, are exactly the woman I want. You are smart, independent, you fight for what you believe. And..." He paused and stepped closer, so close she felt his breath on her cheek, his erection pressing against her thigh. "And you are the woman who makes my heart throb. You are the woman I wish to share my life with."

Moisture pricked Jane's eyes, but she blinked it away. "But your country, your father, your people—"

"Will follow as their leader commands and will love you as I do."

Jane's throat closed. Her heart ached to give into him. To her own feelings and needs and desires.

"I understand you have reservations," he said in a gruff voice. "That you may wish to continue a career."

She nodded.

"And I will respect whatever you choose to do." He stroked her cheek with the pad of his thumb. "Unfortunately we have crimes in Kyros for you to investigate. And then there is the environmental project which I need help with, a spokesperson in particular."

She had been impressed with his plan.

He lowered his lips to her neck. "Although I could keep you quite busy in bed."

Jane's knees wobbled. She was fast losing any reason to deny herself. Stefan was the man of her dreams. Rather, the man she'd never allowed herself to dream about. "Stefan, I just don't want to disappoint you."

He brushed her cheek with his thumb with such tenderness that Jane felt weak.

"Don't you understand," Stefan said in a low voice. "You could never disappoint me." He pressed his hand over his heart. "I will not disappoint you, either, Jane. I love you, and I will do everything in my power to make you happy."

A tear finally trickled down Jane's cheek. Stefan thought she was brave, but she had been such a coward with her heart. She did want him. She did trust him.

Silently acknowledging her feelings gave her the courage to speak them out loud. "I love you, too, Stefan."

A smile filled Stefan's eyes, and he gently wiped the tear away with his thumb. "Those words are magic to my ears, my love." His eyes locked with hers, then he dropped to his knee, and reached inside his pocket.

Jane's belly fluttered with nerves, her heart filled with hope and anticipation.

Stefan held out a simple black velvet ring box, his own hands shaking. "I wish to marry you, my Jane. To make you my wife." He opened the box, and a perfect oval jade stone winked at her in the dim light.

"If you say yes, you can have any ring you select." His voice warbled with emotions. "My mother's, although it is ostentatious. But there are jewelers in Kyros who will design the jewel of your heart's desire."

Jane clung to his hand, unable to speak.

"But this stone will always remind me of you,"

he continued. "Of your beauty and your home, which I hope to also make my own."

Jane stared at the dark, jade stone, the gemstone of Wyoming, so simple in its beauty yet so timeless. And she finally found her voice again. "Oh, Stefan, this is perfect for me. Absolutely perfect."

"As you are for me."

More tears fell as Jane succumbed to her feelings, and he placed the jade on her finger. Then he swept her in his arms and kissed her, and she kissed him back with all her heart.

When they finally came up for a breath, she reached for his hat. "You know, I like you in your crown, Stefan. But there's nothing sexier than a prince in a cowboy hat and boots."

Stefan threw his head back and laughed, and she pushed him to the blanket. Desperate for each other, the picnic basket was forgotten as they rushed to undress each other, stripping and kissing and exploring each other's bodies with frenzied need.

They made love beneath the stars glittering in the Wyoming sky with Stefan wearing nothing but those cowboy boots.

And as she nestled in Stefan's arms afterward, contented, sated, euphoric, her heart bursting with love, she finally believed that fairy tales did come true.

After all, plain Jane was marrying a prince, and they would live happily ever after in a beautiful kingdom called Kyros…

* * * * *

Next month, look for
SEIZED BY THE SHEIK
by Ann Voss Peterson,
the next book in Harlequin Intrigue's
new continuity, COWBOY'S ROYALE!

LARGER-PRINT BOOKS!

GET 2 FREE LARGER-PRINT NOVELS

PLUS 2 FREE GIFTS!

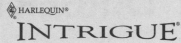

HARLEQUIN®

INTRIGUE®

Breathtaking Romantic Suspense